THE
LEGEND
OF

Mallard
Lake

A NOVEL

JUDITH BLEVINS
& CARROLL MULTZ

Judith Blevins
Carroll Multz

NEW!

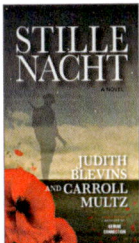

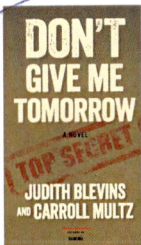

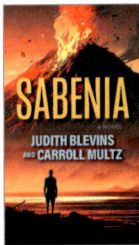

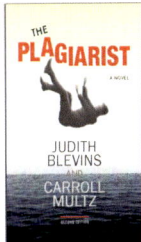

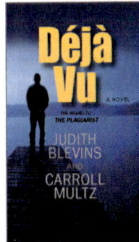

The Legend of Mallard Lake

Published by
ShahrazaD Publishing®
2189 W Canyon Court
Grand Junction, CO 81507-2574

ISBN – 979-889372561-2

Contact the authors at:
judyblevins@bresnan.net
carrollmultz@charter.net

ALSO BY THE AUTHORS

Dedication

To the lost and forgotten.

Opportunity sometimes knocks only once.
Seize it and don't let go!

Blevins & Multz

TABLE OF CONTENTS

A Note From The Authors

First loves seem to be etched in the minds of those of us who are old enough and experienced enough to draw comparisons. Events beyond our control, such as changing towns or schools or induction into the military, account for what may amount to discarding the old and moving on to the new. Love normally does not have time to flourish relative to the previous encounter, and the mantra *out of sight—out of mind* takes on a whole new meaning in a new environment and at a new time. Never mind the adage that *absence makes the heart grow fonder.*

The forbidden fruit concept fuels our longing, and rebellion oftentimes trumps common sense. When the odds are stacked against us, we sometimes throw caution to the wind and gamble all our chips on one roll of the dice. Sometimes we win but most often we lose. Was it worth the risk? It may take almost a lifetime to find out. Buyers' remorse? Who can predict? If we could predict the future, would we still make the same mistakes? If we don't try, we may never know. And if it's tantamount to a curse, we usually have the opportunity to overcome it. But sometimes certain events are beyond our control and unpredictability makes life a mystery and a game.

Special thanks to Jan Weeks for her editing skills, Frank Addington for the cover and interior book designs, and Rosalie Stewart and John Lukon of KC Book Manufacturing for printing The *Legend of Mallard Lake*, and finally to our readers, you continue to be our inspiration.

Prologue

Mallard Lake, a favorite vacation spot for those fortunate enough to afford summer homes, is located at the foot of the Big Belt Mountains and overlooks Prickly Pear Valley close to Helena, the capital of Montana. Explorer Meriwether Lewis was mesmerized by the mountains when he first discovered them. He wrote in his journal:

"...this evening we entered the most remarkable cliffs that we have yet seen. These cliffs rise from the water's edge on either side perpendicularly to the height of 1200 feet. Every object here wears a dark and gloomy aspect. The towering and projecting rocks in many places seem ready to tumble on us.

The river appears to have forced its way through this immense body of solid rock for the distance of 5 3/4 miles and where it makes its exit below has thrown on either side vast columns of rocks mountains high. The river appears to have worn a passage just the width of its channel or 150 yds. It is deep from side to side nor is there in the first 3 miles of this distance a spot except one of a few yards in extent on which a man could rest the sole of his foot. It was late in the evening before I entered this place and was obliged to continue my route until sometime after dark before I found a place sufficiently large to encamp my small party... from the singular appearance of this place I called it the Gates of the Rocky Mountains.

Somewhat flooded today by the backed-up waters of Holter Lake, these Gates of the Mountains are just as magnificent as when the Corps of Discovery first beheld them. Western Montana was founded on placer gold and the Big Belts lent a hand. While the better-known Last Chance Gulch gave birth to Helena, in 1864, three former Confederate soldiers discovered gold in a steep narrow canyon heading east of today's Canyon Ferry Lake and christened the area Confederate Gulch.

Chapter One

The Legend

Seventeen-year-old Miranda McClain, was the only child of Rudy McClain, Helena's banking mogul, and his wife, Lucinda Lancaster-McClain. Lucinda was elevated to a social position when she married the president and owner of the local bank. She considered the nickname 'Lucy' to be disrespectful and soon after the wedding no one dared call Lucinda 'Lucy'. "My name is Lucinda!" she would snap at the surprised offender who was often taken aback by her rudeness. She soon acquired the reputation of being a snob. Living in a mansion on Helena's west side added to the publics' perception as did the family's vast holdings.

Other than being the wife of the president of the bank, Lucinda's claim to fame was having been runner-up for a spot in the first Miss America Beauty Pageant held in Atlantic City in 1921. She was eighteen in '21, and now twenty years later, was still a head-turner. She was often the recipient of wolf-whistles when out shopping. On such occasions, she would smugly flip her hair over her shoulder, pretending to ignore the whistler. However, as she continued her trek down Last

Chance Gulch, Helena's main shopping area, she secretly delighted in still being recognized as a beauty queen.

Miranda was the mirror image of her mother, with a wealth of golden hair, big, innocent blue eyes, and fair skin. Because of her musical talent and athletic ability, she was very popular among her peers.

• • •

For as long as Miranda could remember, the McClains spent their summer vacations at their lodge on Mallard Lake. However, Miranda was never allowed to invite any of her friends to join them at the lodge. The one and only time Miranda asked to bring friends, her mother exploded.

"Absolutely not! Why, those heathens will destroy everything your father has worked so hard to provide for us."

Miranda never understood what her girlfriends could destroy but she didn't dare challenge her mother.

Deprived from interacting with her school friends over the summer, Miranda often felt like an outsider when classes resumed in the fall. However, her effervescent personality and winning smile soon overcame her doubts and she was welcomed back with open arms.

• • •

It was 1941 and that fall would be the start of Miranda's high school senior year. She brooded over missing her last high school summer vacation with classmates, and as she walked around the lake, she absentmindedly tossed pieces of stale bread to the ducks that flocked to the lake. She felt like the Pied Piper as the ducks followed her around the three-mile perimeter. On most occasions, when she was halfway around the lake, Miranda sat down on a wooden bench close to the water. The ducks quacked and waddled around her feet searching for crumbs. When they discovered she was out of bread, they soon deserted her. She was now all alone—an all-too-often occurrence.

• • •

Miranda was deep in thought and didn't notice when a handsome young man slipped onto the opposite end of the bench. When she sensed his presence, she jumped.

Holding his hands up in surrender, he said, "Sorry I startled you. I didn't mean to. My name is Grady, Grady Penwell. I'm staying with my aunt and uncle, the Thorntons, for a few weeks." Pointing up a slight incline behind them, he continued, "Their lodge is right up there."

Miranda smiled, "Yes, I know Thurman and

Vivian. We've been lake-neighbors for many years. My name is Miranda —"

"Miranda McClain," Grady interrupted. "I've noticed you walking every day since I've been here. It gets boring playing cribbage and croquet with the old folks all the time, so I thought I'd intercept you and introduce myself and perhaps walk with you."

Miranda laughed. "After a couple of weeks in this isolated place, everything gets boring."

"Sounds like you could use some excitement," Grady said with a grin. "My uncle has a canoe. Would you like to go canoeing?" he asked.

"Oh, yes, I'd love to, but…"

"But what?" Grady asked, arching his brow.

"But…Mother wouldn't allow it."

"What if she doesn't know?" Grady asked.

"Oh, she'd know alright. She knows everything I do." Miranda sighed. "If she doesn't figure it out on her own, someone is always more than willing to tell her."

"You mean even my Aunt Vivian?"

"Yes. They're close friends and play bridge quite often when my dad is here."

"I see. Wouldn't want to get you in trouble," Grady said. "Walking is just fine. Do you mind if I join you?"

"Not at all," Miranda replied. She was grateful

for someone close to her age to converse with.

As they traversed around the lake, Grady asked, "Have you heard of the legend of Mallard Lake?"

"No! Didn't know there was one. I love legends." Miranda was all ears and Grady could sense the excitement in her voice.

"Even if they don't have happy endings?" Grady asked.

"Yes. Like history, even legends tell a story of the era."

Grady gestured toward an empty picnic table and the two took seats across from each other.

"Okay, out with it!" Miranda said, leaning forward on her crossed arms.

Grady, obviously enjoying building the suspense, finally said, "Last evening, over dinner, Aunt Vivian related the hand-me-down story of a young couple, Willard and Irene. They are said to have met the summer Willard was visiting relatives here at Mallard Lake. And Grady said, smiling at Miranda, "They fell in love!"

"That's not much of a legend," Miranda said tersely, disappointment evident in her voice.

When Miranda started to stand, Grady pointed to her seat, "Hold on! I'm not through," he said and raised his brow. "When Willard left the lake, returning to his home in England, he promised

Irene he'd be back as soon as possible. That was in late 1914 right after the Great War began. It wasn't called WW1 until after WWII began. Because mail was slow in the early nineteen hundreds, it took a while for Willard's relatives to receive word that Willard was aboard the *Lusitania* when it was sunk by the Germans in 1915. When Irene learned of the tragedy, she collapsed, overcome with grief."

"How sad," Miranda remarked, apparently concerned but not overwhelmed. "I still don't see how that became a legend?"

"You're so inpatient!" Grady said wearily. "I'm getting there!" His ingratiating smile softened the reprimand. "Irene became withdrawn and refused to eat. She wouldn't talk to anyone and stayed pretty much to herself. Her parents understandably were concerned and decided it would be best to take her home and get her away from the lake and the memories it held.

"The night before they left, Irene slipped undetected from their cabin. When her parents found her missing the next morning, they launched an all-out search for her. The surrounding neighbors joined in. Someone eventually found a pair of shoes located at the lake's edge. They were identified as Irene's. Although a body was never recovered, it was surmised Irene just walked out into the lake and drowned."

"How tragic," Miranda sighed. "I still don't see—"

Grady held up a hand signaling patience and continued. "For years afterwards, and even today, when the moon is full, there are reports of a 'spirit' walking across the lake at night in the area where Irene disappeared. Of course, it's believed the spirit is that of Irene."

Miranda, now captivated by the prospect and being a romantic at heart speculated that Irene was haunting the lake waiting for her love to return. "What do you think?" she asked, knowing her supposition defied the laws of nature.

"I don't believe in ghosts," Grady said. "The logical scientific explanation is, that when water evaporates, the warm, moist air over the water's surface mixes with cooler air in the atmosphere and creates condensation causing fog to form. I think the imagined spirit is just fog or steam drifting across the lake."

"You would," Miranda teased. "However, I'm going with the spirit theory," she said. Tracing the woodgrain on the tabletop with her forefinger, she added, "I like to think love endures all things." She fluttered her eyelashes and looked at Grady for a response.

"Don't make a flawed rush to judgment," said Grady. "It appears you've been influenced by happy ending movies and novels. Real life doesn't always have happy endings, whether we like it or not."

"You're so practical," Miranda shot back. "Don't you know it's fun to be awed, surprised, and even scared by make believe?" Still looking at Grady, she added, "Try it sometime, you may like it."

"No thanks, I'll keep my feet firmly planted in reality."

Not willing to give up, Miranda pointed to him and said, "Too bad you're so stubborn and unyielding. You're missing some exciting emotions. Heart-stopping moments when Dr. Frankenstein's monster closes in on his prey, shivering in your bed when a werewolf howls at the moon in the middle of the night, sleeping with a clove of garlic tied around your neck to ward off vampires—"

Laughing, Grady threw his hands up in surrender. "Okay, you win. You're too much… and I love it!"

Miranda grinned, reveling in her victory. As they continued their walk, she asked, "Are you still in school?"

"Graduated two years ago and joined the Navy. I come from a long line of Navy men. Growing up, I was, and still am, mesmerized by their war stories. Don't know if it was expected, but it just stood to reason I'd follow suit. I've only been in for six months but I'm thinking of making a career of it. I can retire after twenty years. I'll only be forty then—with nothing but time and money on my hands," Grady said smugly.

"I envy you," Miranda said. "Sounds like you have your life planned."

"It was an easy decision. How about you? Do you plan to go on to college?"

"Yes. My father wants me to follow in his footsteps and become an accountant and eventually take over managing the bank," Miranda said wistfully.

"Uh-huh, and what do you want?"

Throwing caution to the wind, Miranda blurted, "Excitement, travel, being amazed by our world and filled with wonder. I don't want the humdrum life of a banker. Yuck!"

Grady stopped walking, "Take the advice of an older and wiser man," he said, "follow *your* dream, not your father's."

"If only it was that easy…Where are you stationed?" Miranda asked.

Realizing Miranda didn't want to continue the discussion about her career path, Grady said, "Lucked out! I'm assigned to the *USS Arrow* which is part of the Pacific Fleet anchored at Pearl Harbor."

"Wow, you did luck out. I've always wanted to visit Hawaii."

Grady, taking Miranda's hand, and with enthusiasm said, "You should! Opportunity knocks only once."

Although Grady's boldness surprised her, Miranda made no attempt to remove her hand from his as they continued walking.

"Hawaii is a good place to start your heart's desire of 'excitement, travel, being amazed by our world and filled with wonder.' It's like no other place on earth. It's known as the Paradise of the Pacific!"

"My Aunt Agnes lives in Honolulu, and every year in her Christmas card, she invites us to come for a visit. Maybe for my graduation present…"

"When do you graduate?"

"June 9, 1941!"

Grady laughed. "Not only do you have it down to the month and year, but you also have it down to the day." After a pause, he asked, "Don't suppose you know the time?"

"No, but only because it's not yet determined," Miranda replied with a grin. Stealing some of the spotlight, Miranda very casually said, "After all, that's almost a year away."

Grady good-naturedly took her arm and looped it through his and they walked along in silence for a few minutes. As they neared the McClain cabin, Miranda stopped. "It would be better if I'm not seen with you," she said. "Mother—"

"It's all right," Grady interrupted, "I understand. Will you be walking tomorrow?"

Gently pulling her arm free, Miranda whispered, "Yes."

"I'll wait for you—at *our* place!" Grady said and grinned.

"*Our* place?"

"Yes, the bench where we just met."

Miranda nodded and glanced in the direction of the McClain lodge. "I'll be there as close to nine o'clock as possible. If I'm a little late, please wait for me." She hoped her anxiety was not obvious.

Grady saluted and clicked his heels together before turning back toward the Thornton lodge. Miranda giggled at his dramatic exit, then she continued home with a lighter step and a song in her heart. *How sweet, our place. I like him.* She thought about the legend of Mallard Lake and its secret. *Life indeed was precarious.*

• • •

Miranda was wide awake at sunrise. She was so eager to see Grady, the next day couldn't come fast enough. When she arose, she went to her closet and chose a pale pink summer dress and sandals instead of jeans and tennis shoes. Today she took special care with her hair and makeup. She even practiced what she hoped would be the quintessential captivating smile. *First impressions were lasting impressions!*

"My, my, don't we look nice," Tulla, the McClain's housekeeper, exclaimed when Miranda entered the kitchen.

"Thank you, Tulla," Miranda replied, and headed for the dining room hoping to avoid probing questions. Her mother barely looked up when Miranda entered. She absentmindedly stirred a spoon around in her coffee cup, apparently engrossed in the society section of the morning newspaper.

"Morning, Mother," Miranda chirped as she slipped onto her chair at the opposite end of the long dining room table.

"Hmm," her mother responded, still not looking up from the paper.

Tulla entered the dining room and served Miranda a poached egg, toast, and orange juice. "Thank you, Tulla," Miranda said, and glanced at her watch as she spread her napkin on her lap. It was 8:30 and Miranda was anxious to start her walk. She gulped down the juice and took a few bites of toast.

"I'm going for a walk," she said to her mother as she rose and placed her napkin on the table as the grandfather clock in the hall chimed 8:45.

"All right," her mother mumbled, apparently irritated by the interruption. That her mother was introverted when it came to Miranda was no surprise.

· · ·

Miranda noticed the sky was overcast and it looked like rain when she stepped from the cabin. However, nothing could dampen her spirits as she quickly walked the mile to "our place" to rendezvous with Grady. He was already there and jumped up when he saw her coming. Miranda noticed him fold a pocketknife and slip it into his pants pocket. She quickened her pace. When she was close enough, he opened his arms and she rushed into his embrace. Looking up at him, she asked, "What were you doing?"

Glancing down at the wooden bench, Grady replied, "Oh, just a little carving."

Miranda looked down. The initials *GP + MMC* were freshly carved in the wood and encircled by a heart with an arrow through it.

"Now it's officially '*our* place'," Grady said as their lips met.

Thunder roared as lightning streaked across the sky. *Is that an omen?* Miranda wondered.

"I didn't think you'd come because it's going to rain," he said as he held her close.

Peering at the sky, Miranda said, "If we hurry, we can shelter in the old boathouse."

Taking her hand, Grady led the way as they ran to the boathouse. They made it just before the deluge hit. Rain pounded on the metal roof competing with the thunder. It was so loud inside the boathouse, it was impossible to talk. However, words were not necessary. Grady pulled Miranda into a warm embrace and kissed her tenderly. His kiss turned into a passion Miranda had never experienced and she clung to him, eagerly returning his excitement. She knew she was flirting with disaster but couldn't stop. They lay in an embrace until the rain subsided and the morning turned into afternoon. The forbidden was a mystery no longer!

Sensing it was getting late, Miranda jumped up, "Oh, my gosh. I've got to go," she exclaimed as she hurriedly dressed and pulled her hair up into a ponytail.

Taking her hand, Grady said, "I'll walk halfway with you." Before they were close enough to see the McClain cabin, Grady asked in a soft voice, "Any regrets?" Miranda shook her head in reply. "Will I see you tomorrow?" he asked in a tentative tone and raised his brow.

Miranda nodded and slipped her hand from his. Before continuing toward home, standing on her tiptoes, she reached up and kissed his cheek. "Yes, I'll be there tomorrow."

Touching his cheek where Miranda kissed him, Grady smiled as he watched her disappear. Intrigued by the encounter, he yearned for a return engagement.

• • •

"Miranda! Come in here! I want to talk to you!" her mother ordered as soon as Miranda entered the house.

Miranda shook with fright when she heard the tone of her mother's voice. It was that *you're in deep trouble* voice. *How could Mother know?* She slowly walked into the living room and took a seat on the sofa opposite her mother "Yes, Mother. What is it?"

"Vivian Thornton just called and told me she observed you walking, and holding hands of all things, with her nephew, Grady. You know your dad and I disapprove of you seeing older men. It appears you deliberately went against our rules. What do you have to say for yourself?"

In the past, Miranda never contradicted her mother. However, today was different. She pulled herself up unto an erect position and replied, "Grady isn't what you call 'an older man,' Mother.

He's barely twenty. I'm almost eighteen so he's only two years older than I. That's a lot less than the difference between you and Father.

"Don't you talk back to me, young lady," her mother snapped, her face red with rage.

"Sorry, Mother. I meant no disrespect. It's only—"

"Never mind your excuses! Having been away to college for two years and then in the military makes that Grady person an older man. Boys learn things in college and the service that no decent… Well, never mind. I forbid you to ever see him again!" Her mother folded her arms across her chest and glared at Miranda.

Although she expected her mother's tirade and command, Miranda was nonetheless devastated. Her mother's words, "…forbid you to ever see him again" rang loudly in her head and at that moment she resolved to go against her mother's dictate. Miranda was resentful and bitter that her parents kept her away from most school activities and from interacting with her classmates. *I won't let them keep me away from Grady. I'm old enough to make my own decisions.* She vowed she'd find a way.

• • •

The next morning, Miranda went through the usual breakfast routine. However, after breakfast, she told her mother in a muted voice she was going to her room and read one of the books she knew would be a mandatory class assignment in her senior year.

"That's more like it," her mother said. "What book is it?"

"Oh, ahh, *Gone With the Wind*," Miranda replied. "It's rich in history and the culture of the period…"

"So, it is. It's smart to get a jump on your assignments." A frosty smile graced her mother's face and she went back to reading the society section of the newspaper.

It was almost 9:00 o'clock when Miranda left the breakfast table and went to her room. She opened the window and slipped out, closing the window behind her. Instead of taking the walking path, Miranda skirted the back of the lodge and went through the underbrush. When she was sure she was far enough away from the lodge and out of her mother's sight, she made her way to the walking path, checking over her shoulder from time to time to ensure she hadn't been followed. When she saw Grady waiting, she quickened her step. She was breathless when she arrived at what had been designated as *our* place. Grady stood when he saw her coming.

Miranda rushed to his open arms. "This is the last time I'll be able to see you," she sobbed. "Your Aunt Vivian told mother she saw us walking hand in hand and mother forbade me to ever see you again." Still crying, Miranda continued, "I took a chance and climbed out of my bedroom window this morning. I don't think she heard me," she muttered and took a quick look over her shoulder. "I had to see you once again."

Grady stroked Miranda's hair, "I know all about it. Aunt Vivian told me she talked to your mother." Then brushing hair from Miranda's eyes, he said, "I don't want to cause a rift between you and your family, so I decided to leave first thing tomorrow and head back to base." After a brief pause, Grady added, "Obviously, I can't even write to you?" It was more of a question than a statement.

Angerly swiping tears from her cheeks, Miranda blurted, "Yes, you can. I've been thinking about that. I brought my best friend's address. You can send the letters to her and she'll deliver them to me."

Grady shifted from foot to foot, "I don't want to get you in trouble. Are you sure—"

"I'm sure. Charlotte would never betray me. She knows what a domineering person my mother is and thinks Mother treats me unfairly—that's putting it mildly."

Grady rubbed the back of his neck. He finally said, "Okay, it's a deal."

Miranda withdrew a piece of paper from her jeans pocket. "This is Charlotte's address. I wrote it down last night…just in case you agreed to my plan."

Grady glanced at the address then folded the slip of paper and stuck it in his wallet.

Miranda looked around, and trying to camouflage her destress, finally said, "I must be getting back before I'm missed. I'll miss you… don't forget to write."

Grady pulled Miranda into an embrace. He kissed her lips tenderly and she responded. As he released her, he took her hands saying, "Of course I'll write as often as possible. You'll be in my thoughts and prayers constantly." Then glancing at the bench where they spent happy hours together, he said, "When the time is right, I'll meet you back here at *our* place."

Miranda slipped her hands from his, and looking down at the bench where the initials were carved, she traced them with her fingertips and replied, "Yes, our place." She then turned toward home. Before leaving the path and disappearing into the underbrush, she looked back. Grady was still watching. She blew him a kiss and he pretended to catch it in midair and pressed his hand to his heart. Not caring who heard him, he called out, "I love you!" The sudden noise startled a flock of mallards that had been floating about on the lake scrounging for aquatic plants and snagging unfortunate bugs that crossed their paths. The mallards squawked, flapped their wings, and took to flight.

Throwing caution to the wind, Miranda called back, "I love you, too!" and hoped Grady heard her over the noise the mallards were making. It was *not a goodbye but see you later*—an expectation that would never falter.

• • •

Before the McClains left Mallard Lake to return to their home in Helena, even though Grady had left a few weeks prior, Miranda would walk to the bench where they said their last goodbye. She again traced the initials he had etched in the wood with her fingertip and longed for the day she would see him again. Occasionally, Miranda would think of the legend revolving around Willard and Irene. Absorbed in her longing for Grady, Miranda understood how Irene must have felt after she lost Willard. *Wonder if Irene's mother put the kibosh on their relationship like Mother did mine. Hope desperation never pushes me over the edge.*

Chapter Two

Aloha

The summer melted into autumn and Miranda returned to school. True to his word, Grady wrote Miranda almost every day. The only days he missed were the days he was out on maneuvers. Miranda shared her letters with Charlotte, who said they sounded like romance novels. Charlotte was intrigued by forbidden love and relished being part of the conspiracy.

• • •

Although Grady missed seeing Miranda, he found the Navy a good fit for him and he flourished. The *USS Arrow* was a large warship armed with 16-inch guns. Grady was assigned to the crew operating and maintaining the ship's weapons systems. In his letters, he let Miranda know how much he liked being in the Navy even though he couldn't give her any specifics of his duties aboard ship or the ship's location. He also described to her the beauty of the Hawaiian Islands and wished she could be there to see for herself.

Miranda read and reread Grady's letters. She tied them with a blue satin ribbon and kept them bundled up in a shoebox under her bed. Rereading his letters and missing him so much reinforced her desire to visit Honolulu, if for no other reason than to be near Grady.

• • •

Autumn and winter were behind them and spring flourished in Helena. High school graduation was only days away.

"Miranda!" her father bellowed one afternoon, motioning her into his home office. This ritual usually meant Miranda was in trouble. However, she was pleasantly surprised when her father said, "You have made your mother and me very proud of you. Graduating valedictorian is indeed an honor. Remember, we promised you anything within reason for your graduation if you kept your grades high. You exceeded our expectations and now it's time to reward you. What would you like?"

Her father often said, "A man is only as good as his word." Miranda knew her parents would keep their promise, even if it went against their better judgment. Being embolden by her father's sense of honor, she said, "Having given it much thought, I've decided I'd like to visit Aunt Agnes in Honolulu."

"What! Thought you'd want one of those snazzy new convertibles," her father jovially retorted. "However, a McClain always keeps his word." He looked at his wife and she nodded.

"After all, Miranda has been the perfect daughter since we returned from the lake last summer. She earned her reward," her mother said sweetly with a smile. "Too bad we can't accompany her but we've had that month-long cruise booked for over a year. We've really been looking forward to it. Cruising is all the rage now, you know. Because July is the only month available for Miranda's visit since she starts college in August, I'm sure she'll be in good hands with my sister. I'll contact her right away and make arrangements for Miranda's visit."

Aunt Agnes was delighted when she received the call and said she looked forward to seeing Miranda.

• • •

Miranda breathed a sigh of relief when the trip to Honolulu was finalized. She hoped for more time but was grateful for at least a month. After embracing both parents, she went to her room and wrote to Grady outlining her plans. She hoped the *Arrow* wasn't going to be out to sea on maneuvers during July. She knew Grady, of course, couldn't tell her anything regarding the ship's itinerary, but perhaps he could drop a hint.

• • •

The next day the McClain women were in

seventh heaven as they went from shop to shop on Helena's famous Last Chance Gulch. They had a heyday purchasing appropriate attire for their respective excursions. They had so much fun, Miranda enjoyed shopping with her mother for a change. Every so often she felt a pang of guilt about being deceitful regarding the real reason behind her trip but was able to rationalize her actions and the guilt quickly dissipated. *No harm, no foul!*

• • •

The evening before Miranda departed, she and her mother went over a list to ensure Miranda had everything she'd need for the trip. Her mother said she'd be in good hands with Aunt Agnes so they weren't worried about Miranda's health and wellbeing.

The next morning, both parents accompanied Miranda to the airport. After hugs, kisses, and farewells all around Miranda finally boarded the plane. Securely buckled into her seat aboard the Pan American flight, Miranda finally accepted the reality that she was on her way. Grady was foremost on her mind. She had been plagued with a constant thought that it was all a dream and she'd wake up to a sad reality.

Miranda had never flown before and was absorbed in the activity aboard the plane. She admired the stewardess' professionalism. They were polished and performed their duties to perfection. Miranda observed the passengers seated close to her. They appeared to be seasoned travelers, and unlike herself, they ignored what was happening around them and studied the newspaper or thumbed through magazines. Some even snoozed. The distractions made time go by.

It was early evening when Miranda arrived in Honolulu. When she stepped from the plane, she was wrapped in a warm, tropical breeze that smelled like perfume. She had never been to the tropics and the sensation was new and delightful.

Entering the terminal, Miranda spotted an attractive older woman holding a sign with Miranda's name on it. Looking closer at the woman, Miranda could readily tell she was her mother's sister; they looked very much alike. Miranda began waving her hands above her head until she finally got her aunt's attention. Agnes waved back and the two made their way through the throng and embraced.

"My, my!" her aunt began, "You've certainly evolved into a lovely young woman."

"And I'd know you anywhere, you look so much like my mother."

"Thank you. That's quite a compliment

considering your mother was a runner-up in a beauty pageant."

Miranda paused. *Opps. Sour grapes?* Not knowing if her aunt was kidding or serious, she decided to let it go and be more circumspect in the future when it came to mentioning her mother.

"Come. Let's get your luggage," her aunt said with a smile. "I took a taxi since the airport is usually crowded after a flight and getting out of the parking area can be a challenge."

Miranda nodded. Rummaging through her shoulder bag, she finally found her luggage claim ticket. Stepping up to the counter, she handed it to the attendant. A redcap seemed to appear out of nowhere and offered to assist them with Miranda's bags. Once they retrieved the bags, he expertly guided them through the concourse to the outside curb where they secured a taxi. Aunt Agnes handed the redcap a tip. "Thank you, ma'am," he said. Then tipping his hat, he disappeared back into the terminal.

Once they were in a taxi, Miranda couldn't keep from swiveling her head in all directions. The cab driver took a highway that skirted the ocean. She was mesmerized by the landscape. The sun was just setting, and the scene was breathtaking. White capped waves licked the beaches, graceful palms danced in the evening breeze, and as sun slipped over the horizon, red and gold fingers streaked the clouds.

Her aunt lived in a multi-unit apartment complex overlooking the ocean. Her two-bedroom apartment was on the second floor. Barely inside, her aunt said, "We'll call right away and let your parents know you've arrived safely."

Placing her luggage on the floor, Miranda said, "Good idea. Their cruise leaves from Miami, so they're leaving tomorrow for Florida. My final instructions were to let them know I've arrived as soon as I could. I know they're anxious about my traveling alone for the first time."

After making the call to her parents, her aunt showed Miranda to her bedroom. It was facing west and the sun had just disappeared over the horizon. Before unpacking, Miranda slid open the balcony doors and stepped out. From her vantage point, she could see the ocean and even hear the waves crashing onto the shore. Looking down, she noticed a path leading to the ocean. It appeared to be a short walk to the beach. Joining Miranda on the balcony, Aunt Agnes said, "Now you see why I love it here."

"Would you consider adopting me?" Miranda joked.

Agnes chuckled and said, "I have dinner almost

ready. I'll meet you in the dining room in half an hour."

After her aunt left, Miranda reluctantly tore herself away from the balcony, and washed her hands and face. Before leaving her room, she paused at the balcony doors and once again peered at the ocean. She was filled with excited expectation. Spotting a naval vessel in the distance, her thoughts turned to Grady.

• • •

When Miranda entered the kitchen, Agnes was putting the finishing touches on poke, a local favorite Hawaiian dish.

"This smells great," Miranda said as she helped set the table. "What's in it?"

"Very simple to make," her aunt replied. "Tuna, onions, sesame seeds, seaweed, and soy."

Miranda cringed when her aunt said seaweed but she didn't say anything. *After all, when in Rome...* Her apprehension dissolved as soon as she tasted the dish. It was delicious, and Miranda ate two servings.

"Fresh pineapple for dessert," her aunt said as they cleared the table.

"Fresh pineapple sounds great. However, if I eat another bite, I'll explode," Miranda groaned.

"Maybe later," her aunt suggested. "It's still

early. Would you like to walk down to the beach?"

"Yes, I would!" Miranda said enthusiastically. Before leaving for Hawaii, Miranda had sent her aunt's phone number and address to Grady. She had been wondering ever since how she would explain Grady to Aunt Agnes. She hoped the walk would provide an opportunity and her aunt would understand. Then, on the other hand, she might find herself on the next plane headed home.

• • •

The pathway leading to the beach was enhanced with typical Hawaiian flowers blooming on either side. Aunt Agnes, sounding like a tour guide, pointed to the plants and identified the flowers as they traversed the path. When they approached a hibiscus, Agnes stopped and plucked a beautiful pink blossom from the shrub and placed it behind Miranda's right ear. She then explained, "It's a Hawaiian tradition. If you're available, you wear a flower behind your right ear. However, if you're married or spoken for, you wear the flower behind your left ear. Miranda realized her aunt had just given her the opening she hoped for. She stopped and slowly moved the hibiscus to behind her left ear.

Agnes looked at her. "No, dear. You wear the flower behind the left ear if you're spoken for." Agnes then made a move to switch the flower to the right side. Miranda caught her hand in midair. Her aunt gazed at her. "Are you trying to tell me something?" she asked.

"Yes, Auntie, I am."

"Okay, I'm listening," her aunt replied and looked at Miranda with questioning eyes.

Even if her aunt judged her, she was relieved to have someone other than Charlotte to talk to. Miranda slowly related her summer romance with Grady at Mallard Lake. She didn't leave anything out, not even the morning spent in the boat house, and her mother's command that she never see Grady again. Her aunt listened intently.

When Miranda finished her story, she prepared herself for a hailstorm of criticism. Instead, she was stunned by her aunt's reaction.

Her aunt replied, "Well, that explains a lot. I wondered why you chose me over the 'snazzy new convertible.'" Her aunt's humor put Miranda at ease. "Come, let's sit down on that bench over there," Aunt Agnes continued. "I have a story for you, as well."

When they were seated on the bench which faced the ocean, they watched the waves wash ashore for a few minutes. Finally, Aunt Agnes began. "I was a year behind Lucinda. She was the most popular girl during all our high school years.

You know the type, cheer leader, homecoming queen, prom queen, most likely to succeed, et cetera, et cetera. Every boy in school had a crush on her, even the freshmen swooned over her. If a boy was ever attracted to me, she'd lure him away. Why? Not because she was interested in him, but because the boy was interested in *me*.

"After we graduated, I got a job and met a nice young man by the name of Johnny Goodwin. When we began dating. I wouldn't allow Johnny to come to my home and pick me up, knowing he'd probably be lured away by Lucinda. We always arranged to meet elsewhere. Although he never questioned my strange request, I'm sure he wondered what I was hiding. We eventually became serious enough to become engaged. He wanted to meet my parents, and they, of course, wanted to meet him.

"By that time, I was so secure with our relationship, I agreed. Mom suggested I invite him to dinner to meet them. On the day of the dinner, Lucinda was nowhere to be found. I hoped she had other plans and wouldn't show up at all. However, after we were seated at the table, Lucinda made her grand entrance. She must've spent the day shopping for alluring attire, and at the beauty salon. When she waltzed into the dining room looking like a million bucks, Johnny actually dropped his fork when he saw her. "You can guess the rest," Agnes said and sighed.

"Don't leave me dangling," Miranda replied. "What happened?"

Her aunt swallowed hard. She finally said, "Guess you deserve to know. I left home and eventually made my way to Honolulu. I got a teller's job at a bank. Two other tellers, my coworkers, were also on their own. One afternoon over lunch, we agreed to join forces, and sharing expenses, we were able to survive. I was eventually promoted and made enough money to buy this residence."

"What happened to—" Miranda asked.

"Johnny? He got dumped just like all the others. Served him right! I wouldn't say for sure but I think your dad's position with the bank appealed to Lucinda. She always fashioned herself a socialite and never loved anyone but herself. Being married to an up-and-coming banker was right up…" Agnes stopped midsentence and blurted, "Oh, my! I'm so sorry. It's your mother we're talking about! I had no right to…"

Realizing her aunt's distress and reluctance to reveal family secrets, Miranda took her aunt's hand, "It's all right. You haven't told me anything I didn't already suspect," she said in a consoling voice.

Agnes nodded. "Don't take me wrong. I love

your mother. After all, we are sisters, but there were times when she could be trying."

Now it was Miranda's turn to nod. "How well I know!" she said. "How well I know!"

Her aunt stood. "It's getting late. We should go back." As they retraced their steps, her aunt asked, "How did you plan to meet with Grady here in Honolulu?"

"I'm sorry, but I took the liberty of sending him your phone number. He knew I'd be visiting my aunt. I hope you don't mind."

"Of course not," her aunt replied, then added, "I trust you'll be more discreet and not take chances," she said sternly and looked squarely at Miranda.

Miranda knew she was referring to getting pregnant. "I've lived with guilt for over a year. Talking to you eased my mind. However, I'm not going to get back into that situation. Grady and I agreed to wait until we were married to…to…"

"Got it!" Aunt Agnes replied. "You'll be glad you did." She then stared into space as if remembering a difficult time and place, and after a moment she shook her head. "Not everything has been peaches and cream," she murmured.

Chapter Three

Fleet's In

As the days passed, Miranda became anxious at not having heard from Grady. *I wonder if I've made a complete fool of myself in coming here.*

Agnes watched Miranda pace, twisting a tissue, occasionally dabbing at her eyes during the week as Miranda fretted and speculated as to why Grady hadn't called.

Hoping to console Miranda, her aunt said, "It's not unusual for the fleet to be out to sea for a week or more. Even though we're not at war, the Navy operates as if we were. Being prepared is tantamount to victory."

"I know, but—"

"Patience, my child. What will be, will be."

"I'm only here for a month and time is running out. What if the fleet stays out for the entire month?"

"Highly unusual," Agnes said, although she didn't know that for sure. She wanted to reassure Miranda.

• • •

The next day, the *Arrow* finally docked at Pearl Harbor. The first thing Grady did, after the ship was secure, was call the number Miranda provided.

"Hello," Agnes answered when the phone rang.

"Hel…hello, Miss Agnes," Grady stuttered. It was apparent he was nervous.

"Yes, this is Agnes."

"Ah, my name is Grady Penwell. I'm a friend of Mir—"

"Yes, Grady. We've been expecting—" Before Agnes could finish her sentence, Miranda grabbed the phone.

"Grady! Is it really you?" she shrieked.

"Miranda, yes, yes, it's me!"

"How soon before I can see you?" Miranda asked.

"Unfortunately, not until tomorrow afternoon. We have debriefing—"

"Hold on," Miranda interrupted. "Aunt Agnes is trying to tell me something."

"Ask him if he can come to dinner tomorrow evening." Agnes said.

"I overheard your aunt's invitation. Tell her it would be my pleasure. What time?" Grady asked.

"Six o'clock," Agnes said loud enough for Grady to hear.

"I'll be there," Grady replied.

Suddenly, Miranda heard a cacophony of voices in the background on Grady's end of the phone. "I've got to go. My shipmates are clamoring for the phone," Grady said. "Until tomorrow…"

"Yes, until…" the phone went dead.

Miranda was so giddy with happiness, she jumped up, and taking her aunt by the hands, began to involve her in a modified version of ring around the rosie.

Agnes smiled. *Ahh! To be young again.*

• • •

The next evening, when it was close to 6:00 o'clock, Miranda began pacing. As she passed the dinner table, she checked the place settings and rearranged the silver service for the umpteenth time. Passing the mirror in the entryway, she fussed with her hair. She adjusted the straps on her sundress, smoothed the skirt and continued pacing.

Aunt Agnes motioned for Miranda to simmer, but to no avail. *My goodness, I hope that boy shows up soon.*

In true military fashion, Grady was right on time. Miranda was in the foyer when the doorbell rang, and flinging the door open, she wrapped her arms around Grady's neck. Grady pulled her into a warm, gentle kiss. Aunt Agnes could see the couple from the kitchen doorway and tried to look inconspicuous as she busied herself putting the final touches on dinner. Taking Grady's hand, Miranda pulled him into the foyer.

Drying her hands on her apron, Agnes stepped briskly from the kitchen. "Auntie, this is Grady!" Miranda said and smiled broadly.

Grady stepped forward and extended his hand. "I'm pleased to meet you," he said nervously.

"And I you," Agnes replied, as the two shook hands. "Come make yourself comfortable while I put the finishing touches on dinner."

"How can I help?" Miranda offered.

"Thank you, dear. You keep our guest company," Agnes responded.

After a brief conversation between Grady and Miranda regarding Grady's Navy career and Miranda's journey to Hawaii, Agnes returned to the room, and motioning to the dining room, announced dinner was ready.

• • •

The mood was cheerful and the conversation around the dinner table was lively. Grady was bombarded with questions regarding his military service, and he graciously answered the ones he could.

"With the war raging in Europe, I hope you understand there's certain things we're not permitted to discuss," he said and shrugged.

"Of course," Agnes acknowledged and placed

her napkin on the table. "If we're finished here," she said and looked at Miranda, "why don't you take Grady for a walk down to the beach while I clean up the dishes?"

"Oh, no. I'll help with the—" Miranda began.

"Nonsense. Now, get on out of here!" Agnes ordered and made a shooing motion with her hands.

Miranda stood. "Guess we've got our marching orders," she said to Grady as she grabbed his hand and pulled him up from his chair.

"Yes, ma'am," Grady said politely. "Thank you, Miss Agnes, for the wonderful dinner."

"You're welcome. We'll have dessert later, pineapple upside down cake."

• • •

As Miranda and Grady walked toward the beach, a gentle breeze ruffled the palm fronds.

"This is the first time I've been to the ocean," Miranda said as they strolled hand in hand down the path.

"And what do you think?" Grady asked. "It's not quite Mallard Lake, but—"

"Love it! I could stay here forever," Miranda said as she held tightly onto Grady's hand.

"That can be arranged. I'll smuggle you aboard the *Arrow* and let you get a taste of the other side of paradise," Grady joked. "I can teach you to sleep in a hammock."

"Is there a downside?" Miranda asked.

"Naw, not after you get over seasickness, irregular exhausting hours, an ill-tempered captain who is never satisfied, cramped quarters, and dealing with bad weather, just to name a few inconveniences, life's a breeze." Grady took a deep breath.

"Oh, my. I had no idea," Miranda replied, her mouth agape.

Stopping, Grady took Miranda into his arms. "However, I wouldn't trade it for anything. I love the Navy and serving my country. With everything that's going on in Europe, one wonders how much longer we'll be on the fringe. I'll take a ship compared to a foxhole or jumping from a plane any ole day."

Miranda let go of his hand and nestled in his embrace. "Grady, I'm afraid…"

Miranda tilted her head and Grady tenderly kissed her on the exposed cheek. "Don't be. We're prepared for the worst, but hopefully we won't have to test our strength." After a few minutes, he added, "I should be getting back to the ship. We're on strict shore leave orders while docked at Pearl. I believe your aunt said something about pineapple upside down cake."

"Indeed, she did."

Aunt Agnes had the table set for dessert when the couple returned from their walk. "It's sure nice to have home cooking," said Grady as he took his seat and caught a glimpse of the mouthwatering dessert.

"The pleasure is all mine," Agnes replied.

Having talked of war while they were walking put a damper on Miranda's spirits and she was unusually quiet. *What if we do go to war?*

As she served the cake, Agnes said, "You'd think pineapple upside down cake originated in Hawaii."

"You mean it didn't?" Grady asked, picking up his fork.

"Even with tropical ingredients like coconut, banana and macadamia nuts, I understand in 1920, after Dole introduced canned pineapple in the States, a woman from Norfolk, Virginia, won a recipe contest for her original pineapple upside cake," Agnes said and smiled.

Grady nodded as he finished the last morsel, "This recipe would be hard to beat."

After indulging in dessert, Grady again thanked Agnes for the dinner and rose to leave.

Miranda stood and walked him to the door. "Will I see you tomorrow?" she asked unsure he would still be in port.

"Absolutely. Pack your swimsuit and lunch. I'll be here around eleven." He then gently kissed her. "Until then," he said, then left. After closing the door behind Grady, Miranda leaned against the door and glanced at her auntie who was all smiles and gave her a thumbs up.

• • •

Miranda and Grady spent the next three weeks frolicking in the ocean and exploring Honolulu. They knew they were on borrowed time. They snorkeled with the turtles in the bay, waded in the surf, and soaked up the sun as they reclined on beach towels on the white sand that seemed to expand forever. The hypnotic sounds of the swells as they crashed against the beach made them feel that external bliss was indeed forever.

They took tour buses to historical sites. One of the most fascinating was Punchbowl Crater. They learned from the bus driver that the crater was formed over 70,000 years ago. Much to their surprise, the Hawaiian name translates to "Hill of Sacrifice." History tells us that the name refers to the crater being used as an alter for human sacrifice to the Polynesian gods as punishment for those violating cultural beliefs.

"Who would have thought in this paradise that human sacrifice was practiced?" Grady mused.

"Which just goes to show you never know what man is capable of," said Miranda. "The road to hell is paved with good intentions. I'm sure they thought they were doing the right thing. Let's not dwell on the negative and get depressed." Both thought about the legend of Mallard Lake despite the disparity in seriousness between human sacrifice and suicide. Neither, however, mentioned the uncanny similarities.

Grady nodded. "What would you like to do with the rest of the afternoon?"

"Before I leave Honolulu, I must do some shopping," Miranda replied. "I promised to bring Charlotte a gift from Hawaii. She's been so loyal and accommodating as our go between. I'd like to take my parents a gift as well."

"I agree and I know just the place," Grady said. "The bus I take to Honolulu passes by it every day."

• • •

Miranda was delighted with the small boutique. She went from display to display, mulling over what to get Charlotte and her own parents. The puka shell jewelry was inviting, as well as the traditional muumuu dresses. However, the arrangement of wind chimes was the most intriguing. The glass chimes were painted with palm trees, seashells, ocean scenes, and hula dancers. Holding one up so that it tinkled in the slight breeze flowing through the shop, Miranda exclaimed, "Oh, look, Grady. Charlotte would love this."

Noticing the glint in Miranda's eyes, Grady surmised she, too, would love a wind chime. Motioning to the clerk, Grady said, "We'll take two of these."

"Two?" Miranda questioned.

"Yes, one for Charlotte and one for you. How 'bout your mother?"

"Hmm, maybe something more sophisticated."

The clerk, overhearing the conversation, pointed to a display of monkey pod bowls. "Perhaps your mother would like a monkey pod salad bowl with serving pieces?"

Looking at the stacks of polished wooden bowls, Miranda exclaimed, "Perfect! Mother would love them."

After selecting a set for her mother, Miranda looked at the clerk. "Any ideas for my father?"

"Most kāne don't leave islands without an aloha shirt. We have many," the clerk said. "Follow me."

As they followed the clerk, Gardy whispered to Miranda, "Kāne is Hawaiian for male."
Miranda smiled and nodded.

Upon reaching the shirt section, Miranda was overwhelmed. There were so many to choose from, she finally asked Grady to pick one. He sorted through the stacks and finally came up with a fairly conservative one.

"This looks like a banker," he chortled.

Miranda rolled her eyes. "He probably will never be seen in public wearing it but…"

After paying for their purchases, Miranda and Grady left the boutique. Walking to the bus stop, Miranda's happiness was overshadowed by the thought that time was running out and she would be leaving soon. Grasping Grady's arm, she said, "I'll treasure the wind chime forever. It will remind me of you when we're not together," she whispered as tears filled her eyes.

• • •

Miranda's parents phoned regularly upon returning from their cruise. They missed her and were eager for her to return. Even though this was the first time Miranda had been away from home for any length of time, she was surprised that she didn't miss home or her parents. School starts the first week of September," her mother reminded her, and reassured her that she had been accepted and enrolled for the following school term. Her parents agreed to cover the expenses that were not covered by her scholarship. She would be living at home and commuting back and forth. Although she had preferred living in a dorm, her parents wouldn't hear of it. *Once I gain my independence, things will be different. Until then...*

Chapter Four

Double Trouble

One day, after spending the afternoon with Grady, and returning to her home away from home, she found the residence eerily empty. "Aunt Agnes," she called. No answer. As she pondered where her aunt could be, Miranda was suddenly startled when the doorbell rang. She rushed to the door and opened it to find one of their neighbors standing in the hallway.

"Hello, Miss Bethany—" she said looking past the visitor expecting to see her aunt in the hallway.

Bethany cut her off midsentence, "Oh, Marinda. It's just awful," she sputtered.

Fear gripped Miranda. "What's just awful?" she asked.

"Agnes fell down the stairs and I think she has a broken hip."

"Oh, no. Where is she?"

"I called an ambulance and they took her to Honolulu General."

"How long ago?"

"Two hours, more or less," Bethany replied.

Grabbing her purse from the table in the foyer,

Miranda exclaimed. "I've got to go…"

"I'll drive you," Bethany offered.

• • •

Miranda waited anxiously outside the emergency room. When she was finally allowed to see her aunt, Agnes was woozy from being sedated. She held tightly onto Miranda's hand.

"Auntie," Miranda said in a soft voice, "you're going to be just fine. However, the doctor said you would be incapacitated for a few weeks. Because of your age, you suffered a compound fracture that's going to take longer than normal to mend. I'm going to make arrangements to stay with you for as long as you need me."

Tears trickled down Agnes' cheeks. "Thank you," she whispered as her eyes slowly closed and she drifted off to sleep.

Reassured her aunt was in good hands, Miranda checked with her aunt's doctor regarding the amount of time of hospitalization and care after she was released. Upon hearing the type of care that would be involved, she knew she could perform the required duties. She suddenly felt a pang of guilt at being happy she was given the opportunity to stay in Hawaii to help her aunt, but mostly to be with Grady longer than planned.

The first thing Miranda did when she returned

to her aunt's apartment was to contact her parents.

"Mother," she began. "I'm sorry to be the bearer of bad news. Aunt Agnes fell down some stairs today and broke her hip."

"Oh, no—"

"She's going to be okay, however, she'll need help while recuperating. Since I'm here, I volunteered to stay until she can function on her own."

"What! You did that without our permission!" her mother scolded.

"Yes," Miranda said firmly. "I could not in good conscious leave her now. We're family and I felt an obligation—"

"Miranda, it's okay! I apologize for my outburst. I'm at my wits end. It's been pretty hectic here at home. I, too, have some bad news and didn't want to tell you sooner. Your father is in the hospital. He contacted strep throat and it evolved into scarlet fever. He's expected to recover but it'll take weeks." Miranda's mother paused, "During the examination, his doctor also discovered your father has a heart murmur."

"Oh, no! Do I need to be there?" Miranda asked.

After a long pause, her mother said, "I don't think so. Most heart murmurs are not life threatening. He'll be in the hospital for at least another week. I have Tulla here to help me when he's released. We'll most likely be quarantined by the Health Department because scarlet fever is very contagious. I agree, you should stay and help Agnes." After another pause, "You know this means you'll have to postpone college until the January semester!"

"I thought about that," Miranda responded. "When I start the January term, I can take additional courses to catch up so I can graduate on schedule."

Her mother's voice softened. "Of course, you can. You've always been a good student." Her mother paused, "Tell Agnes we're praying for her recovery. I miss you; you take care of yourself as well."

"I will, Mother. And you, too."

The "I love yous" would have to wait for better times. Miranda couldn't remember her mother ever saying, "I love you." Those words were not in her mother's vernacular, at least where Miranda was concerned.

• • •

The next week was devoted to preparing for her aunt's return from the hospital. Miranda made sure the kitchen was well stocked using the money her aunt provided. With Grady's help, she moved some furniture items to allow room for a wheelchair to navigate through the rooms.

One afternoon before Agnes was released,

while helping Miranda prepare for her aunt's homecoming, Grady took her hand. "I won't be around for a while, I'm sorry to say," he said.

Although Miranda expected it was getting close to time, and although Grady couldn't say so, Miranda knew this meant the *Arrow* was going out to sea on maneuvers. Taking a deep breath, all she could say was, "I'll miss you!"

The couple prolonged their goodbyes. Finally, looking at his watch, Grady exclaimed, "I've got to go or I'll miss my bus."

Miranda slowly walked Grady to the door. Standing in the open doorway, he held her hand for a moment before continuing down the corridor. Before disappearing, he turned and blew her a kiss. She returned the gesture. The scene was reminiscent of the last time they parted at Mallard Lake. Miranda stifled a sob. *'Til we meet again, I'll hold you in my heart.*

After Grady left, sitting alone in her room, Miranda noticed the packages from the gift boutique that were still on her dresser. She opened the small package, and taking out the wind chimes, she carefully placed the one for Charlotte in her overnight case. Taking the other wind chime, she went out to the balcony, and standing on a chair, suspended it from a hook. As soon as she released the chimes, they tinkled merrily in the slight breeze. The tinkling reminded her of Grady and the unspoken promise of a future together.

• • •

The next few months were filled with nursing her aunt back to health. Bethany visited on a regular basis and helped Miranda with the more difficult tasks that required lifting Agnes and transporting her to meet medical appointments. She also ran errands such as filling prescriptions and purchasing supplies.

Miranda and her mother kept in close touch by telephone. Sensing that Miranda was emotionally drained, her mother's twisted view of her daughter began to evaporate. Her intolerance was soon replaced by positive reinforcement and her criticism by praise. Miranda's unselfish indulgence in the care of Agnes and tending to her aunt's special needs earned her her mother's respect, although belated. Miranda's attempt to solidify a relationship with her mother was finally coming to fruition. In fact, her mother's hostility towards her abruptly ended. *One down, one to go.* Miranda had reference to her parents' acceptance of Grady.

• • •

It was the end of November before Grady returned to Pearl. The first thing he did was to contact Miranda.

"Miranda, what a relief to hear your voice," said Grady in a muted tone. "I wasn't sure you'd still be here. I missed you."

Miranda could hear loud voices in the background. "Oh, Grady. I missed you terribly. I'm so happy you're back," Miranda said. After a pause, she added, "Are you in or out of port? Sounds like you have company."

"We just docked, and everyone is clamoring for the phone."

"When can I see you?" Miranda hurriedly asked, afraid someone would take the phone from Grady before they finished their conversation.

"Unless you hear from me sooner, sometime tomorrow. Have a debriefing in the morning. Not sure how long it will last, but I'll be there as soon as possible. By the way, how's Aunt Agnes?"

"Doing much better. She's also anxious to see you."

The phone suddenly went dead and Miranda stared at the receiver before hanging up. However, she had the information she wanted and her heart leapt for joy. *Grady's back!*

• • •

The next day at 11:15 a.m. Aunt Agnes' telephone rang. Miranda answered.

"Put an extra plate on the table. I'm on my way. The debriefing was short and sweet and I'm eager to see you."

"Fantastic! Aunt Agnes is almost as anxious to see you as am I—almost!" Miranda looked over at her aunt who was sitting snuggled in a quilt on an easy chair listening to Marinda's side of the conversation.

Aunt Agnes gave her the thumbs up sign, expressing her whole-hearted approval. It was obvious she was bored with the restricted circumstances following her accident and welcomed company, especially from Grady for whom she was developing a great affection.

"Who knows, he may become a member of the family!" she said as Miranda returned to her side, all grins.

"If only Mom and Dad shared your enthusiasm. They have no idea that Grady is back in my life and if they did, they would disown me and hire a hitman to eliminate the tempter."

Aunt Agnes blanched. "That's quite a stretch. They just don't know Grady like we do."

"They don't want to. They're stubborn and at one time had tried to sway me in the direction of Kevin Randolph, the son of one of Father's old college buddies. He's a spoiled brat who only thinks of himself and someone I would not be caught dead with."

"Does anyone like him?"

"Certainly not me! He's a complete buffoon. Mother would have me marry any ol' bozo if it elevated her social position."

"I see your point," her aunt said. "It's been my experience that matchmaking usually results in disaster. I take it Grady was and is the man!"

"For all seasons. However, I don't want him to come between me and my family. I respect them too much to do that. Even now, going behind their backs, I feel guilty. I love Grady and I love them. I'm caught, as they say, between a rock and a hard place." Then looking forlorn, Miranda sighed, "Please, Aunt Agnes, tell me what to do!"

"Miranda, we've had this discussion before. Having been conflicted myself, I know what you're going through. If only I had the answer. You go against the wills of your parents, you risk alienating them. If you capitulate to your parents' demands, you risk losing the love of your life."

"Mother's solution is her mantra: 'There are other fish in the sea.'" Miranda shook her head. "In my case, there's only one."

"Sounds like Lucinda. If the shoes don't fit, try another pair," Aunt Agnes remarked. "She was an expert at changing shoes."

Miranda chuckled. "That's a good analogy. However, I've never liked fishing or trying on shoes."

Now it was Agnes' turn to chuckle. "Touché. As you've gathered, only once in my life have I loved. By following my parents' wish, I let my heart be guided by their absurdity and I suffered the consequences. To this day, I still consider Brad *numero uno* and someone I will unite with in the hereafter. Brad is the one I dream about."

"And him?"

"Wherever he is and whatever he's doing, I'm sure he's not forgotten me either. He, too, was heartbroken when we parted. I can't forget the look on his face and his reaction when I told him I couldn't see him again. I know he was confused by my tears and my reaction whenever we ran into each other. It was apparent to him and everybody who knew us that I was still in love with him."

"Did you get a chance to compare notes and tell him the untold story?"

"Much like you, I didn't want to override my parents. I knew if we huddled together that would ignite the relationship and neither of us would risk losing the other. I knew I would not be strong enough to let go."

"How old were you then?"

"Close to eighteen."

"Would it have made any difference if you had been old enough to go out on your own?"

"Same dilemma! To break the cycle of control would mean bye-bye family. I was tempted to throw caution to the wind and elope, and Brad had the same frame of mind. I know he did, because he had been hinting about marriage and his desire to be married in the Catholic Church which was something my parents would have been adamantly opposed to. I know, because I discussed it with my parents just before graduation. I guess they correctly surmised things were serious between Brad and me."

"Wow! Just what I'm now facing with Grady," Miranda blurted.

"Has he proposed?" Aunt Agnes asked.

"Not in so many words."

"How do you feel about overriding the wishes of your parents and running with your heart? I grew up with your mom and know she usually gets her way."

"I have been rebuffed, belittled, humiliated, and controlled by my mother my whole life. I don't feel I owe her anything."

"I think you've answered your own question."

Chapter Five

Surprise Attack

December 7, 1941, 7:48 a.m. Terror rained from the sky as the Japanese executed their surprise attack on Pearl Harbor. The Navy base at Pearl was their main objective but they didn't hesitate bombing other targets of opportunity such as manufacturing and distribution facilities on the island.

A massive explosion rocked Agnes' apartment, throwing Miranda out of bed. She stood just as another explosion shook the floor. She staggered toward her aunt's bedroom, shouting for Agnes. The living room curtains were open, giving her the first view of the devastation as Japanese planes screamed overhead. More bombs fell. Terrified out of her wits, she ran to Agnes' bedroom. "Auntie, what's happening?" she shouted.

Her aunt was sitting on the edge of her bed rubbing her face with her hands when Miranda barged in. "I don't know," she replied. "It sounds like the fleet is engaging in war games again. But with more vigor."

Miranda ran to the bedroom window. "Oh, no!" she exclaimed. "I think this is the real thing. I see a lot of black smoke and flames in the direction of Pearl Harbor."

Just then a bomb exploded close to their building. Miranda screamed. A moment later she was helping Agnes slip into her shoes and urging her to flee. "Come on, it's not safe here."

"But—" her aunt started to protest but was silenced by more bombs exploding all around them. She quickly pulled on her robe as she limped toward the door. "Where will we go?" she shouted as they made their way down the stairs.

"Don't know, but staying inside doesn't seem like a good idea," Miranda panted.

When they exited the building, they were swarmed by a mass of panicked people running helter-skelter. Miranda and Agnes were absorbed into the mass and pushed along by the momentum of the mob, headed toward the beach. Not knowing what to do to protect themselves, they went with the flow. However, because of Agnes' inability to keep pace with the crowd, the two fell behind.

When they reached the beach, Agnes collapsed onto the sand, burying her head in her hands. Escape appeared unlikely. Miranda was at a loss as to what to do. She sat down beside her aunt and put an arm around her shoulders to give her reassurance and to comfort her. Suddenly, Miranda observed a figure approaching them from the opposite direction. She recognized him to be a native Hawaiian. Gripped with fear, she stood up, but not before grabbing a rock that was embedded in the sand beside her. However, upon closer inspection, he appeared to be harmless and Miranda relaxed.

"Do not fear, I'm a friend," he said as he came closer. "It's not safe for you to stay here."

Looking up and down the beach, Miranda said frantically, "I know, but what are our choices?"

"Come. I'll take you to a safer place," he answered.

Can we trust him? Looking down at her aunt, Miranda said, "My aunt can't walk very well. She's recovering from a broken hip."

"I'll get help," the native said and motioned to someone behind him. When the second man approached, the first native explained the situation. Then the two locked arms to create a two-person carry and lowered their arms to accommodate Agnes. Miranda helped her aunt stand and she was gently eased into the seat the men had made with their locked arms. Sweat poured from the two men's brows. Agnes placed her arms around their necks and the four of them cautiously walked toward where open air first aid stations were in the process of being established. They could feel the concussions of the explosions.

The air was thick with smoke and it was hard to breathe. They could smell the burning fuel from exploding ships. The aid stations were crowded with people covered in blood as they waited their turn. Pain and anguish were evident from their moans and cries. Medical people were harried and hurried, and hope, it appeared, was rapidly dwindling. Maybe first aid stations were not a safe haven after all.

Miranda knew the *Arrow* was anchored at Pearl. Her concern, now that Agnes was safe, was for the ships in the harbor, and of course, Grady.

• • •

Later, the military reports disclosed that seven of the nine battleships assigned to the Pacific Fleet were docked at Pearl Harbor at the time of the attack. The fleet's flagship, *USS Pennsylvania,* dry docked at a nearby Navy yard, was hit only once damaging some of her guns. She sustained only minor damage. The other Pacific Fleet ship absent from Pearl at the time of the attack was the *USS Colorado.* She was being overhauled in the States. The battleship, *USS Arrow*, not an official member of the Pacific Fleet, was also anchored at Pearl when the attack occurred. By the time the attack was over, most if not all of the ships docked at Pearl

Harbor had sustained major damage.

The diabolical attack lasted an hour and fifteen minutes. Not only was the Pacific Fleet almost completely destroyed, but the attack also severely damaged two American airbases, Hickman and Wheeler Fields. The city of Honolulu had also been shelled. With a population of approximately 180,000, miraculously, only 49 civilians were killed and 35 others wounded during the attack.

• • •

Most of the injured treated at the first aid stations were military personnel because the ships sustained direct hits, their sickbays, for the most part, were inoperable. The injured reclined on cots, gurneys, or the ground, many screaming in pain or moaning, begging for help. The nurses moved from patient to patient performing triage.

• • •

It seemed like an eternity before a team arrived and moved Agnes to a cot beneath one of the first aid canopies. Once her aunt was comfortable and stabilized, Miranda said, "Aunt Agnes, you're in good hands now and you'll be safe here… at least for the time being." She then looked around. It was obvious there weren't enough able bodies to tend to the injured. "I can't just sit here. I'm going to volunteer to help wherever I can," she said to her aunt.

Agnes managed a meager smile. "Just don't forget where you left me."

Miranda kissed her aunt on the forehead. "I won't," she whispered. "I promise!"

• • •

Volunteers, mostly lay people, were utilized to help during and after the attack. There wasn't time for sanitizing, either hands or wounds, the volume of patients was so great. A doctor, identified by his name tag as Dr. Benjamin Roye, stopped briefly by Agnes' cot to assess her condition.

"I'm Miranda, and this is my Aunt Agnes," Miranda said, "she's recovering from a broken hip." She then asked, "How can I help?"

"Your aunt appears to be stable." Then, without looking up, the doctor said, "I can use an assistant. Grab my bag and stay close to me."

Thankful for at last being able to do something useful, Miranda followed the doctor from patient to patient, carrying his medical bag. Although she didn't know medical terminology, she was soon able to figure out what the doctor needed by just observing and using common sense. She worked at the doctor's side the rest of the day and into the night. When they finally took a break and went to one of the food tents, she was near collapse. As they sat at a picnic table, Miranda noticed that the breeze reeked of smoke and burning petroleum instead of the usual scent of tropical flowers. In a little over an hour, the thriving paradise had been transformed into hell.

Soon after they sat down, a volunteer brought them hot coffee and sandwiches. "Thank you," the doctor said to the volunteer. Then turning to Miranda, as he bit into the ham sandwich, asked, "What's your last name?"

Miranda peered at the doctor over the rim of her paper coffee cup. For the first time, she noticed how handsome he was, even with five o'clock shadow. She guessed him to be in his late twenties to early thirties. His dark hair was cut military style and his piercing blue eyes looked through you, not just at you. "McClain, Miranda McClain," she replied, returning his stare.

"Well, Miss McClain," the doctor continued, "you handled yourself quite well. Not too many non-medical, or even medical individuals, could have performed as well as you under the circumstances. Have you had medical training?"

"I just graduated high school, and I think I've been running on adrenaline. Please call me Miranda. My aunt," Miranda said, nodding toward the first aid tents where she left Agnes, "lives here in Honolulu. This vacation was a graduation present from my parents before I go on to college."

After a moment of silence, Dr. Roye asked, as he popped the last bite of his sandwich into his mouth, "Where's your home?" He wiped his hands on a paper napkin, folded his arms on the table, and leaned forward staring into Miranda's eyes as he waited for her to answer.

Feeling uncomfortable under the doctor's close scrutiny, Miranda shifted and cleared her throat before saying. "Helena, Montana."

"Hmm, never been to Montana but hear it's a beautiful state. California is my home. After graduating from medical school, I wanted to serve my country. Although we weren't at war, because of my love for the sea, I joined the Navy. I was assigned to the *USS California* which was the only ship anchored at Pearl at that time. I thought I was one lucky son-of-a-gun..." The doctor's eyes shifted toward the first aid tents and looking melancholy, added, "Little did I know—"

Miranda interrupted. "I have a friend serving aboard the *Arrow.* Is there any way to find out if he—"

Before Miranda could finish the sentence, Dr. Roye shook his head, apparently anticipating the rest of the question. "Too soon after the raid to expect any information. Also, I suspect that traffic in and out of the islands will come to a halt, including air traffic." Rubbing the back of his neck, the doctor mumbled, "I think we're officially at war with Japan."

A sailor approached. "Dr. Roye! You're needed in the surgery tent—"

The doctor immediately rose. "I'm right behind you." He looked at Miranda. "Think about a career in the medical field. You're a natural."

Miranda spent the rest of the night on a cot next to her aunt. Her last thought, before drifting off to sleep was of Grady. Was he injured? Did he survive the attack?

The next morning the buildings that weren't damaged by the bombing were cleared and the residents were allowed to return home. Other than a few items having been dislodged from the walls, Agnes' residence was virtually untouched by the air raid. From the balcony, Miranda could see a nearby radio tower hanging at an angle—a reminder of the ferocity of the attack. She shuddered, remembering the horror.

• • •

The doctor was right. Congress declared war on Japan on December 8, 1941, and Germany declared war on the U.S. January 13, 1942. Suddenly the United States was thrust into World War II, fighting the enemy simultaneously on two fronts. *Remember the attack on Pearl* was the rally call of the new military recruits. Many patriots enlisted in the service of their country. Many were drafted. The time between boot camp and deployment to the front lines was truncated. Necessity and the survival instinct made them instant heroes. And as one general pointed out, "There are no atheists in fox holes."

. . .

Defense measures were mandated. Military personnel from the Army and Navy were stationed around the perimeter—some on ships; others on land—of the Hawaiian Islands, and metal and concrete barriers were erected on the beaches to obstruct any landing effort on the part of Japan. The U.S. Army controlled the airports and all commercial and private planes were grounded.

Martial law was instituted and with it came curfews, blackouts, and other restrictions including censoring the news and mail, both incoming and outgoing. The Hawaiian Islands essentially became a military base. All residents were fingerprinted and required to carry identification cards with them at all times. It was initially thought that martial law would last a short time. Unfortunately, it spanned three long years.

• • •

Miranda didn't want to be tagged as a spy because of her extensive probing following the attack. She finally gave up her quest to determine what happened to Grady. Trying to track critical locations and personnel might be misconstrued. Censorship was deemed critical to our national security and no one was above suspicion. *Funny how the despicable actions of a few could affect so many!*

Grady, by being in the military and thus isolated from his loved ones, especially Miranda, was the litmus test of their love for each other. It would test their resolve. How long would they be apart? How long would they have to wait—each not knowing what the other was thinking? Circumstances beyond their control lurked in the shadows.

THE LEGEND OF MALLARD LAKE— JUDITH BLEVINS & CARROLL MULTZ

Chapter Six

Stranded in Paradise

The *USS Arrow* was docked at Pearl Harbor and most of the crew were in the mess hall eating breakfast when the Japanese attacked. Sirens pierced the air and the gun crews scrambled to return fire. Grady and his crew clambered to the deck and began firing the 16-inch cannons at the Japanese Zeros. That's where they were when the ship was hit by a Japanese bomb causing the stern to explode. Sailors were blown off the deck and parts of the ship were damaged beyond recognition. The bomb missed the main part of the ship, but nonetheless, still caused considerable damage. Debris became airborne and Grady was struck on the head by a piece of flying metal.

Several seamen came to his aid and moved him to a safe place. Although Grady didn't have any severe external injuries other than a bump on his head, he seemed to be disoriented. He squinted at the seamen as if he didn't recognize them. His shipmates noticed he was unable to focus, his movements were slow, and he seemed to be uncertain as to where he was or what he was doing.

When he spoke, he was incoherent and quivering as he held his head with both hands. He ground his teeth and grimaced in pain. His head pounded and a sizable knot began to form on his forehead.

"We better get Grady to sick bay," one of the seamen said. "I don't like the way he's acting. It's not normal. Let's hope he doesn't have a concussion!"

Two seamen lifted him, and hustling him across the listing deck, escorted him to the ship's hospital. The facility was in a state of chaos. It was crowded, disorganized, and in disarray. With the influx of injured crewmen, it was obvious there were too many injured and too few doctors.

Ignoring the usual protocol, a doctor asked, "What's the injury?" when the threesome entered.

"Don't know, he became confused after we were hit by a bomb. He was struck on the head by a hunk of metal torn from the deck and now he just seems to be disoriented and confused," one of the seamen replied.

The doctor did a quick exam. He probed Grady's head with his fingertips. "He has a pretty good-sized bump," the doctor said, and took a penlight from his breast pocket and studied Grady's eyes. When the doctor asked Grady questions, Grady was non-responsive and unable to remember anything. For example, when Grady was asked his name, he just shook his head.

"From what you tell me and from what I've observed, it appears he has a concussion."

• • •

Ambulances were lined up on the dock at Pearl Harbor to transport the injured to the hospitals in Honolulu. Grady was placed in the passenger seat of one of the ambulances leaving the ambulance bay area open for the more critically injured and transported to the nearest field hospital. He was assigned a cot in a tent with the least injured. Resting on his back, he stared up at the tent top. His head hurt, and he was still confused as to who he was and what was going on.

"Seaman, I'm Dr. Evans," the doctor stated as he approached Grady's cot. "I'm going to examine the wound on your head."

"Dr. Evans, where am I?" Grady asked and looked around.

"You're in a field hospital tent in Honolulu."

"Honolulu? I don't remember…" Grady's voice trailed off. A moment later, he asked "What's my name?"

Looking at Grady's dog tags, the doctor responded, "Grady Penwell. Does that ring a bell?"

Grady Penwell. Grady furrowed his brow and thought for a moment. He finally said, "No. What happened?"

The doctor continued to scribble notes on Grady's chart. Without looking up, he replied, "While manning the guns on the *Arrow* during the attack, you were hit on the head with a piece of debris when the ship was struck by a bomb. My initial examination reveals you have a temporary loss of memory."

"How long is 'temporary?'" Grady asked with a hint of panic in his voice.

"Hard to say," Dr. Evans replied. "People recover differently. In the meantime, I'm going to keep you here for observation. When it's safe to leave the islands, I'm recommending the Navy return you to the States for follow-up treatment."

Grady looked away. "What if I don't regain my—"

"Patience, lad. I have no reason to believe you won't," Dr. Evans said. The doctor placed his pen in his breast pocket and turned to leave. "I'll be back later," he said. "I'll have the nurse give you a sedative to help you, so try to relax."

"Thanks, Doc," Grady whispered and pulled the sheet up to his chin. *Try to relax,* was his last thought before drifting into a restless slumber.

• • •

A few days after the attack, when telephone

service was restored, Miranda called home.

"Hello," her mother answered, anxiety evident in her voice.

"Mother, it's Miranda—"

"Miranda! Oh, thank God. We've been frantic with worry. Are you alright?" Miranda could hear her mother call to her father, "Rudy, it's Miranda."

"I'm okay, shaken and stunned but physically unharmed," Miranda managed.

Through a series of sobs, her mother replied, "We've been waiting on pins and needles…"

"I know. Telephone service has just been restored and I phoned as soon as I could. We are under martial law and have many restrictions."

"What kind of restrictions?" her mother asked.

"All residents have been fingerprinted and are required to always carry identification cards with them. We're subjected to blackouts and curfews. Even our mail is censored."

"Oh, my! How soon will you be allowed to come home?" her mother asked.

"We haven't received any information regarding travel, so I don't know. There's a great demand for medical personnel here now. I was thinking of getting a nursing degree at one of the local colleges instead of waiting to resume my studies when I return home."

"What! Are the colleges even open? And do you think you'll have to stay there for four years?"

"Although Honolulu was hit pretty hard, a lot of institutions are resuming business. Aunt Agnes is getting around on her own now and I can't just sit here and basically do nothing."

"I don't know…" her mother started to protest.

"If things change and I can leave before I finish a degree here, I can have my credits applied to a college in the States."

Miranda heard her father in the background demanding, "Let me talk to her!" Apparently grabbing the phone, he shouted in a loud voice, "Miranda! What's all this nonsense about nursing school?"

"Well, hello, Father. How are you feeling?"

"Never mind that!" her father growled. "I want to know what you're doing over there and why you can't come home."

"Father, travel is restricted. No one knows for how long. I don't want to put college off another semester. At this rate, I'll be an old woman before—"

"And when did you decide to become a nurse?" her father interrupted. "We thought you were leaning toward an accounting degree to eventually take my place as president of the bank."

"That's what *you* decided," Miranda corrected. Her words were harsher than she intended and she immediately regretted her insolence. Rubbing her brow, she continued in a more conciliatory tone, "I've been helping in the field hospitals since the attack and taking care of Aunt Agnes. I have a knack for nursing. I can get a nursing degree in two and a half years at a local college. Aunt Agnes said I could stay with her for as long as needed."

"Oh, for Pete's sake! Hold on," her father blurted. Miranda heard him conversing with her mother but couldn't make out what they were saying. When he came back on the line, he said, "Your mother and I agree that might be a good idea after all since you can't leave and are still caring for Aunt Agnes. Let us know when you get something lined up. Here's your mother."

Well, father's attitude hasn't changed much. Curt and to the point!

A moment later, her mother was back on the line, "You should not be faulted for standing up for yourself and making a career decision of your own choosing. Don't be deterred by your father's tirade. Nursing is a noble profession and having a nurse in the family is a good thing. Besides, what would Agnes do without you?"

From the background, Miranda heard her father

grunt, "Humph!" She could imagine the argument her parents would probably have after the call.

Unabashed, her mother continued, "We'll, of course, arrange for your tuition and repay Agnes for your room and board—even if she protests."

"Thank you, Mother."

"Give our love to Agnes," her mother said. After a pause, she added, "It's pretty empty here without you. Take care of yourself and keep in touch."

"I will. Love you both!"

Her father had been stone cold towards her for the most of her life and she still called him by the formal designation. "Dad" was not warranted nor permitted. She did not have disdain for her father— only admiration and respect. Grady was and would always be the irrefutable male figure in her life— someone who accepted her for what she was. She was her own person, not her mother's clone nor her father's puppet. She carried her parents' genes but was not their pawn nor easily manipulated. She kowtowed to their tantrums and edicts all her life. Those days were over and a bright new future was dawning.

Chapter Seven

Lost But Not Forgotten

After the attack on Pearl Harbor and not having heard from Grady, Miranda was stymied in her attempts to find out what happened to him. She was, by not being married, or otherwise related to him, not privy to any confidential information. Although she was downcast, she held out hope that, if at all possible, Grady would contact her as soon as he could. She was sure he hadn't been killed during the attack because a list of the deceased was posted and his name was not on it.

• • •

The new year brought new hope. Having made the decision to attend nursing school, Miranda applied for and was accepted into the fast-track nursing program at Paradiso University in Honolulu. Earning a degree was important to her. However, staying in a place where she believed Grady would be able to find her was more important. That was the main reason she wanted to stay in Oahu as long as she could. A secondary reason was her Aunt Agnes who was still recuperating and in need of someone to care for her. Besides, she had grown in her affection for her aunt and her aunt was her pillar of strength. It was a symbiotic relationship wherein both parties benefited. Miranda provided physical support to her aunt, and her aunt provided her mental and emotional support.

• • •

Miraculously enough, the university had been spared when Honolulu was bombed. Paradiso's campus was landscaped with flora indigenous to the islands. A circular cement path and several wrought iron benches surrounded a fountain which was situated in the middle of a large, immaculately manicured park. In some ways, it reminded Miranda of Mallard Lake.

The university was within walking distance of Aunt Agnes' apartment. Although Miranda could take a bus, she opted to walk most days.

The accelerated nursing program was designed with back-to-back classes. Miranda had little time in between, so she usually took a sandwich and piece of fruit for lunch. One afternoon, as Miranda sat on one of the park benches close to the fountain on the university's campus eating her lunch, a man stopped and spoke to her. He looked familiar but she couldn't place him.

"Say, aren't you Miranda McClain?" he asked. Looking up, Miranda created a visor with her hand to block the sun. "Yes, I am," she replied.

"Dr. Benjamin Roye," the man said with a broad smile.

"Oh, yes, of course," Miranda said and blushed. Placing a foot on the opposite end of the bench, Dr. Roye leaned forward and rested a forearm on his knee. "I'm a guest lecturer here from time to time. I'm on my way back to the hospital and thought I recognized you. Mind if I join you?" he asked and sat without waiting for an answer. Looking at the stack of medical books piled next to Miranda, he said, "I see you took my advice."

"Indeed, I did," Miranda answered. "Helping you after the attack on Pearl sparked my interest in medicine. You just gave me the shove I needed. I enrolled in the accelerated program. I've completed two years and will graduate in six months."

"Six months? Wow, time flies. What are your plans after graduation?"

Miranda looked down at her hands which were folded in her lap. "My father is in poor health, so I'll go back to Helena and help my mother. I'd like to stay here but…"

"But duty calls?" Then looking at his watch, Dr. Roye exclaimed as he stood, "I must run. Hopefully, I'll see you again soon."

"Yes, I hope so, too." As Miranda watched

Dr. Roye walk away something inside her stirred. *He's even more handsome than I remembered!* Just thinking that made her feel guilty. Her true love was lost but not forgotten. The memory of Grady would loom forever.

• • •

Miranda buried herself in her studies to keep from thinking of all the things that could possibly have happened to Grady that would account for his disappearance. She also thought of Dr. Roye from time to time, fascinated but conflicted. Every school day she managed to have her lunch on the bench where she and the doctor had their last encounter, obviously hoping to see him again. Much to her disappointment, he didn't reappear. *Maybe* it's just as well!

• • •

The last six months of schooling passed like a whirlwind. Before she knew it, she was graduating with a nursing degree. Her parents arranged to fly to Honolulu to attend her graduation. Although her father was still having heart issues, his doctor okayed him to fly. Not having seen her parents for three years, Miranda was apprehensive but excited. On the day of their arrival, she and Aunt Agnes met them at the airport.

Their reunion was emotional, punctuated with

tears, hugs, and kisses. Miranda was shocked when she saw her parents. Although her mother looked the same, her father had aged considerably. Miranda's first thought upon seeing the decline in her father was that his days were numbered. She felt a sudden pang of guilt at having defied him by electing to become a nurse instead of a banker. *How could he possibly forgive her?*

Because her mother and aunt hadn't seen each other for over ten years, and knowing what she now knew, Miranda watched them intently as they reunited. Both women cried openly.

"You haven't changed a bit," Agnes said to her sister through her sobs.

Miranda's mother dabbed at her own tears, "Maybe not on the outside," was all she could manage.

When her father embraced her, he held more tightly than usual, and said, "Good thing you became a nurse, I'm going to need one." He then had a coughing fit. Her mother removed an inhaler from her tote and handed it to her husband.

Miranda's emotional high dissolved. *Guess my future has been decided for me.*

• • •

It had been three years since the bombing and Honolulu had rebuilt. Little physical evidence of the destruction remained. Since Agnes had only two bedrooms, the McClains opted to stay at a nearby hotel.

"Your father doesn't sleep well and we thought it best…" her mother explained, as she watched out the passenger side window taking in the tropical beauty.

Miranda nodded. Having witnessed her father's coughing fit, she understood their reasoning.

"Where can we take you?" Agnes asked. If she was disappointed her sister opted not to stay with her, it didn't show.

"The Waikiki," Miranda's mother replied.

Of course. The fanciest hotel in Honolulu, Miranda thought. *Maybe things haven't changed that much after all.*

"Agnes, if you haven't planned dinner, would you like to dine at the hotel?" Miranda's mother asked, still gazing out the window.

"That would be lovely," Agnes replied even though she had planned dinner. Miranda detected a hint of disappointment and maybe some resentment in her aunt's voice. She knew her aunt had meticulously planned the dinner menu and the two of them took extra care to ensure the apartment was immaculate enough to pass the white glove inspection.

When they drove up and parked at the entrance

of The Waikiki, a hotel employee greeted them. He took charge of their luggage. Before exiting the car, Miranda's mother asked, "Does seven o'clock work for you?"

"Yes. We'll be here. Shall we meet you in the lobby?" Agnes asked.

"Of course," Miranda's mother replied as she stepped from the car, and taking Miranda's father's hand, the two headed for the lobby of the hotel.

• • •

On the drive to her aunt's residence, Miranda said, "Doesn't appear that anything has changed over the past three years. Just the same old, same old!"

Agnes patted Miranda's hand, "Don't fret. It's just your mother's way. She must always have the best of everything—and the last word."

Miranda sat in silent reflection. She finally said, "You remember, the Thorntons who have a cabin close to ours on Mallard Lake?"

"Yes, I remember," her aunt replied.

"The Thorntons are Grady's aunt and uncle. I was hoping they may have shared some information with my parents regarding Grady."

"Wonderful! Why don't you ask?" Agnes replied. "It can't hurt."

"Oh, no! Not after Mother forbade me to ever

see him again. I'm afraid if I broach the subject, she'll become suspicious."

"Hmm, perhaps I can finesse—"

"Oh, no! Mother is much too intuitive. She'd see right through that. I don't want to cause a feud and spoil my graduation. Thank you for offering."

• • •

Miranda and Agnes were waiting in the lobby when Miranda's parents appeared. Her mother looked like a million bucks in a new, Hawaiian-style sundress. After greeting Miranda and Agnes, she turned and led them to the restaurant.

"I made reservations when we checked in so we won't have to wait," she said. "Follow me." Miranda, together with her father and aunt, dutifully obeyed.

The maître d' welcomed them. When Miranda's mother told him they had reservations, he quickly scanned a list. Apparently satisfied, he said, "Yes, madam," and snapped his fingers, summoning a waiter.

"Please escort this party to table number thirteen."

Miranda's mother shook her head and pointed to a vacant table by the window.

The waiter looked at the maître d', apparently seeking approval to switch tables. The maître d' nodded, and the waiter led them to the table by the window.

The dining room at The Waikiki was five-star luxurious. Miranda stared at the exquisite appointments in wonder. She had never seen anything quite like it. Round tables draped with white cloths were discreetly separated, allowing diners to converse with each other without fear of being overheard by fellow diners. Hurricane candle centerpieces were the focal point of fresh floral arrangements at the center of the tables, and plush red velvet chairs encircled the tables. Overhead, dazzling crystal chandlers provided low light while soft music wafted though the venue. The waitstaff sported red military-style waistcoats with brass buttons and black trousers.

When everyone was seated, the waiter circled the table handing each one a menu.

"Bring us a bottle of chardonnay," Miranda's mother said without looking up from the menu.

"Yes, ma'am," the waiter said, as he backed away from the table.

Examining the entrees, Miranda's mother asked, "Agnes, since we're new here, what do you suggest?"

Agnes stiffened. *Dammit! Whatever I suggest won't be to her liking and I'll never hear the end of it.* "Well," she began. "I've never dined here before so I hesitate to suggest anything. However, everything looks enticing."

"Hmm," Miranda's mother replied. "Rudy's on a strict diet. The grilled salmon sounds good."

Miranda's father nodded. "I think I'll have that, too."

Taking the hint, Miranda also ordered the salmon. However, the renegade in Agnes reared its ugly head, and throwing caution to the wind, she rebelled and ordered deep fried shrimp and scallops.

"That's a lot of cholesterol," her sister scolded, as she rearranged her silver service.

"I know, but I'll take my chances," Agnes replied in a devil-may-care manner, and spread her napkin on her lap.

Miranda's father was oblivious to the conversation. However, Miranda cringed. *Are they going to create a scene right here in the restaurant?*

The two sisters appeared to be over their snit as the waiter served the salad and refilled the wine glasses. Conversation was light as they ate. As soon as they finished their salad, the waiter reappeared. As he was clearing the dishes from the table preparing to serve the entrees, a gentleman walked up behind where Miranda was seated.

"Good evening," he said, obviously addressing Miranda.

Miranda turned. The surprise on her face was evident. "Dr. Roye!" she blurted. Then regaining her composure, she continued, "Ahh! Let me introduce my parents and my aunt. My parents just flew in from the States to attend graduation."

"A pleasure to meet all of you," Dr. Roye said as introductions were being made.

Miranda's mother smiled sweetly and asked, "Won't you join us?"

Looking across the room, Dr. Roye answered, "Thank you very much, but we," and he gestured toward where his party was seated, "that is, me and some of my fellow professors are also celebrating the end of the semester." He looked back at Miranda, "When I spotted you, I wanted to say hello. I'm giving the commencement address and I was afraid tomorrow would be hectic and I wouldn't have the opportunity to speak to you after the ceremony." Miranda smiled. "My classmates are pretty geared up, so I suspect you're correct," she said meekly. Dr. Roye stepped back and addressing Miranda, asked, "What are your plans after graduation?"

Miranda looked thoughtful for a moment before replying, "I'm going back to Helena and putting my degree to work." However, her voice lacked enthusiasm.

Just then the waiter reappeared with the entrees.

Dr. Roye backed away to give the waiter space to serve. "It was nice meeting all of you," he said. Then to Miranda, "Good luck. Perhaps our paths will cross again." He turned and the four stared after him as he strode away toward his table.

With eyes still focused on Dr. Roye, Miranda's mother whispered, "What a handsome young man, and a doctor to boot." She arched her brow and gave Miranda a look that said, "This one's a keeper."

Miranda picked up on the implication but ignored her mother's comment. *Mother would just love to have a doctor, and professor to boot, for a son-in-law to brag about to her snooty friends back in Montana.*

· · ·

As they indulged in the entrees, the conversation turned to Helena. Agnes asked, "Were many of the servicemen from Helena involved in the attack on Pearl?"

Miranda's mother looked thoughtful. "Yes, a few were aboard the Arizona. A list of the deceased was posted in the newspaper. However, I didn't recognize any of the names."

"Hmm. Did you know any of the families of the boys stationed in Hawaii?"

Miranda coughed and hoped she didn't show her sudden reaction. She glared at her aunt.

"Only the Thorntons. They're neighbors up at Mallard Lake. I believe their nephew was in the Navy." After a pause, she added, "We haven't seen them for a couple of years. With Dad's declining health and the war, we don't go to the lake as often as we used to."

Miranda watched her mother closely. She remembers the summer Grady visited and she's getting suspicious. Eager to change the subject, and hoping to evade further scrutiny from her mother, Miranda said, "All this talk of the war is depressing. Let's talk about something else."

"Of course," Agnes replied, apparently realizing she almost let the cat out of the bag. The rest of the dinner was devoted to sights to see and things to do in Hawaii.

• • •

When they arrived home after dinner, Miranda spent the rest of the evening packing. She retrieved the wind chime from the balcony and carefully sandwiched it in between her clothing. As she snapped the suitcase closed, she was suddenly overcome with sadness. Packing the wind chime was like breaking the last tie to Grady. *If he's alive, why hasn't he contacted me?* She knew she couldn't ask her mother about Grady for fear she would evoke her mother's ire.

●●●

Thankfully, the next day dawned bright and sunny—no rain clouds threatened to spoil the occasion. The commencement ceremony was held in the late afternoon in the university park with the fountain in the background. A stage was set up and adorned with indigenous flower arrangements. Folding chairs were positioned on the lawn for the graduates and attendees. The front three rows were roped off, designated for the graduates.

The venue was buzzing with conversation as the attendees waited for the festivities to begin. However, all conversation ceased when, at the appointed hour, the university band began playing the traditional *Pomp and Circumstance* ushering in the graduates. The grandeur of the venue was so touching, many of the attendees, not to mention graduates, openly cried.

Dr. Roye's address was dynamic and inspiring. He congratulated the graduates on their choice of vocation and wished them a satisfying and fulfilling future. "Satisfying in that it meets your needs and fulfilling at having developed your natural gifts for the betterment of mankind. The world needs more medical personnel, especially now with a war raging across the globe. Your chosen profession is a difficult one, but one you can be proud of. Wear that nurse's cap with pride." At the conclusion of his address, Dr. Roye received a standing ovation just before the sky was filled with mortarboards as the graduates flung their caps into the air accompanied by hoots and cheers.

• • •

Unbeknownst to Miranda, as a celebration dinner, her Aunt Agnes had arranged for the family and several of Miranda's friends and fellow graduates to attend a luau at the Lalaini, a popular restaurant that featured outdoor, private parties. The Hawaiian word luau means coming together for a meal which is enhanced by music and hula dancing. The Lalaini was the perfect venue.

As the sun was setting, native dancers performed vibrant routines to the beat of lively cultural music. The experience was highlighted by traditional Hawaiian dress, including grass skirts, worn not only by the entertainers but by some of the guests as well.

Seated on the grass next to her aunt, without taking her eyes off the performers, Miranda exclaimed, "Oh, Auntie, this is delightful. Thank you so much—for everything."

Her aunt squeezed her hand in reply. Words were not necessary.

Later in the evening, some of the dancers

enticed Miranda and her friends to join them. Grass skirts were placed around the girls' waists and leis hung around their necks. The girls kicked off their shoes and were soon doing the hula like professionals. The warm night was filled with gales of laughter and good-humored teasing among the amateur dancers. Agnes noticed that her sister even joined in the dancing and seemed to enjoy it as much as her younger counterparts. Agnes wished she had been physically able to participate.

It was getting late but the guests were having so much fun they hesitated to leave. The party raged on until midnight and finally broke up. Exhausted, but happy, the McClains, including Aunt Agnes, headed for home. Miranda's parents were dropped off at their hotel with a promise to pick them up at 10:00 the next morning in time to catch their noon flight back to the States.

On the drive home, much to Agnes' surprise, Miranda began to cry. "What is it?" she asked, with concern evident in her voice.

"Oh, I don't know," Miranda sobbed. After a pause, she blurted, "Yes! I do know. I don't want to leave here. Being here is the only real happiness I've ever known. I'm going to miss you terribly."

"And I you," Agnes replied, choking back tears of her own. A moment later, she added, "You know, you're welcome to stay…"

Swiping tears from her cheeks, Miranda said, "With Father on the brink, they're obviously counting on me and I can't let them down."

Agnes reached over and clasped Miranda's hand. "I expected no less from you." After a pause, she added, "It's an open invitation if you ever decide to take me up on it." Miranda was too emotional to reply.

Chapter Eight

Home

When the McClains pulled into their driveway, Miranda was swept back into time, and not all of it was pleasant. It had been a little over three years since she left, and much to her amazement, nothing significant seemed to have occurred. The interior of the family home looked and smelled like it always had when she lived there. The enticing aroma of Tulla's apple pie permeated the air, exciting memories of her childhood as Miranda stood in the foyer. She kept telling herself to concentrate on the good and discard the grudge she harbored concerning her mother. If it hadn't been for her mother, Grady would be more than just a fond memory. Forgiveness apparently was not in Miranda's genes.

Miranda was snapped back to the present when Tulla burst from the kitchen. "Miranda! My baby! I missed you so…" and Tulla's strong arms were suddenly wrapped around Miranda, squeezing the breath from her.

"I…mis…missed you, too," Miranda managed to say as she struggled for air.

Miranda's mother entered the house behind Miranda. Without a hello or other form of greeting after being gone for a week, addressing Tulla, she said, "Take Miranda's luggage to her room."

When Tulla bent over to pick up one of the suitcases, without thinking, Miranda blurted, "Never mind, Tulla. I'll do it," and glanced at her mother. *Nothing's changed.* She then realized she had put Tulla on the spot and covered by saying, "I mean, I'm on my way up so I can take them. Thank you anyway, Tulla." Overriding her mother was a no-no. There was a penalty for that, usually immediate!

Her mother remained surprisingly silent, and busied herself fussing with Miranda's father who came into the house behind her, struggling with a suitcase. Tulla instantly went to his aid and delivered the luggage to the master suite. She also had learned the hard way not to interfere with the lady of the house's *instructions.*

• • •

Alone in her room, Miranda began to unpack. When she pulled the wind chime from her suitcase, she became melancholy. *Oh, Grady. I miss you so much.* She then remembered the letters she had hidden under her bed. *Oh, my gosh! I hope Mother didn't find them.* She instantly fell to her knees, and pulling up the bed skirt, searched for the shoebox. It wasn't there. Her heart skipped a beat, but someone knocked on her door before she could panic. "Yes," she said in a shaky voice.

"Miranda, it's Tulla." When Miranda opened the door, Tulla handed her the shoebox. "I saved these for you," she said. "It's our little secret." She winked and smiled.

"Thank you," Miranda whispered. Relief and emotion were evident in her voice.

Tulla affectionately squeezed her hand. "Your mother asked me to tell you dinner in thirty minutes," she said, then turned to leave.

"Wait," Miranda said and motioned for Tulla to come into her room. Miranda closed the door and turned to face Tulla. "Why do you put up with it?" she asked. "Your reputation is exceptional and you could probably get a better job—working for people who appreciate you."

"Simple answer, you," Tulla replied.

"Me?"

"Yes, you. When your mother brought you home from the hospital, she handed you to me and said, 'Here, you take care of her.' It was love at first sight. You were my baby and I cherished you and loved you with all my heart."

"I had no idea…"

"For what it's worth, I was delighted. You were the light of my life," Tulla said.

"I always thought of you as mother. *You* were always there when I needed help. Always! You taught me how to tie my shoes and brush my teeth. You patiently helped me with my homework. I remember how you made posters using my crayons to show me how a number times another number worked. It was you who got me through my piano lessons and dancing classes." Miranda paused and wiped tears from her cheeks. Then taking Tulla's hands in hers, said, "Don't know how I would've grown up without you. *You* deserve my love and respect—and much more."

The encounter grew awkward. Fussing with the tie on her apron, Tulla looked back at the closed door and said, "I must go see to dinner."

Placing a restraining hand on Tulla's arm, Miranda whispered, "Tulla, I want you with me always. If and when I get a home of my own, I'm hijacking you away from this place."

Tulla nodded, then left the room.

Watching Tulla descend the wide staircase, Miranda breathed a sigh of relief and a prayer of thanks as she caressed the shoebox, pressing it close to her heart. Sitting down at her vanity, she opened it. It appeared all the letters were still there, undisturbed, tied in a blue silk ribbon. She touched them affectionally but couldn't bring herself to reread any of them. It would be too painful at this point not knowing whether Grady was alive or dead.

Since she had no balcony, Miranda looked around her room searching for a place to hang the wind chime. She finally decided and placed a thumbtack above the mirror on her vanity and hung the wind chime. Even if it didn't tinkle, at least it was where she could see it every morning and evening. She smiled, remembering the afternoon Grady purchased it and the happy times they spent together. She replaced the box under her bed and continued unpacking.

• • •

Knowing she was entering dangerous territory, over dinner, Miranda told her parents that she intended to apply at the local hospital for a nursing position.

"What! You can't do that. What about your fath…" her mother started to say but stopped midsentence. She didn't want Miranda's father to obsess over his anticipated bumpy road to recovery.

"I'll be only ten minutes away if you need me," Miranda pledged. "I'm eager to put my degree to work and at the same time assist in Father's care."

After a moment, her mother nodded. "Of

THE LEGEND OF MALLARD LAKE — JUDITH BLEVINS & CARROLL MULTZ   115 course. I'm proud of you, Miranda, and so is your father. Obviously, we hope you will continue to reside with us and continue to call this your home."

Feeling guilty remembering her recent conversation with Tulla, Miranda looked down and said, "Of course."

• • •

There was an urgent need for medical personnel and Miranda had no trouble securing a position at the local hospital. She was assigned to assist in the operating rooms and soon became a skilled surgical nurse. Because of her home situation, her supervisor scheduled Miranda to work the day shift so she would be home at night to help with her father who at this point was pretty much bedridden.

One afternoon when she returned home from the hospital, as soon as she closed the front door, she heard voices coming from the living room. The stranger's voice sounded familiar, but she couldn't place it.

"Miranda, come in," her mother called to her. "We have a surprise visitor."

When Miranda entered the room, the visitor stood. Miranda instantly recognized him. It was Dr. Benjamin Roye. "What a nice surprise," she exclaimed as they shook hands. "What brings you to Helena?" Miranda asked, glancing at her mother, who was all smiles.

"Looking for work," Dr. Roye said in a joking manner. Miranda raised her brow. "I'm officially out of the Navy and exploring new frontiers," Dr. Roye said now in a more serious tone. "While thumbing through a medical magazine, I saw an advertisement for doctors at Helena General. And…as you can see, here I am."

Before Miranda could reply, her mother stood and said, "Dr. Roye is staying for dinner. I'll go help Tulla and take your father his tray. Now, if you'll excuse me…"

Dr. Roye stood. However, not taking his eyes off Miranda, he said, "Of course."

"Can…can I help?" Miranda stuttered as her mother walked to the doorway.

"No, dear. You entertain our guest," her mother chirped as she left the room.

Suddenly, Miranda was out of her element and feeling uncomfortable. She was mesmerized before and was mesmerized now. Dr. Roye was tall, dark, handsome, articulate, and intelligent. Miranda sat, transfixed. *Could it be? Maybe just maybe love is* more *wonderful the second time around.*

After her mother left, regaining her composure somewhat, Miranda gestured for Dr. Roye to take a seat and she slid onto the sofa close to him. "I'm glad I took your advice," she said. "I'm a surgical nurse at General…and I love it—thanks to you."

"I knew you would…you're a natural." Casually placing his hand over hers, he said, "I have an interview with the board tomorrow morning, and who knows, if all goes well, we may be working together. Say a little prayer."

Miranda didn't move her hand as she said, "Well, I certainly hope you get the position. I would put a word in for you, but I'm not high enough on the totem pole to impress anyone."

"You impressed me," Dr. Roye said, grasping both of her hands and looking deep into her eyes. Before he could finish his thought, Miranda's mother came back into the room announcing dinner was served. Dr. Roye rose and offered Miranda his arm. Miranda's mother smiled her approval as the two strolled into the dining room arm in arm.

• • •

Dinner conversation was mostly directed toward the doctor. He regaled them with his exploits and his open personality was punctuated by his keen sense of humor. After dessert, Dr. Roye reared back in his chair, "My gosh, where does the time go? I feel like I've dominated most of the conversation. Hopefully, you don't consider me garrulous like a couple of lawyers I know."

"Nonsense," Miranda's mother said. "We've enjoyed every minute of it."

"You're too kind," Dr. Roye replied and glanced at Miranda.

Did he just blush? Not wanting to embarrass him, Miranda looked down.

Miranda's mother rose, and placing her napkin on the table, said, "It's still early and a lovely evening. Why don't the two of you go for a walk." Miranda scowled at her mother. *It's obvious what she's up to. Now she's matchmaking. With Grady it was just the opposite. If things work out with the good doctor, it will be because of her. If they don't, guess who will be blamed. With Mother, I just can't win.*

• • •

What is more romantic than a walk in the moonlight? However, with someone other than Grady, things were not the same for Miranda. She longed for the palm trees and all things Hawaiian—especially Grady. She also missed Aunt Agnes and her words of consolation and encouragement. Dr. Roye was a *friend*—nothing more; nothing less.

As they strolled down the lane leading from the residence, they spotted the North Star. It was brighter than all the other stars. "Make a wish," Dr. Roye coaxed. "And don't tell me what it is, otherwise, it won't come true."

Miranda suddenly remembered the childhood chant, *"Star light, star bright, first star I see tonight, I wish I may, I wish I might have the wish I wish tonight.*

By now the two had quit walking and were captivated by the brightness displayed by the North Star. "How is it our creator favored that one, out of the millions, to defiantly strut its stuff?" Miranda asked, her gaze transfixed on the standout and the inconsequential stars surrounding it.

"You'll have to ask someone much smarter than me," Dr. Roye replied. "Do you need an answer before making your wish?"

"Not if you can guarantee me that my wish will come true."

"Try it and see!"

Miranda then made her wish that no harm had or would come to Grady and that someday soon he would be making contact with her letting her know he was coming home. Since it had been over three years since she last heard from him, she pondered the unlikelihood that she would see Grady again and what she would do if her lost love was never found.

"It's taking a long time to make your wish," said Dr. Roye impatiently. He secretly hoped it included him. He was smitten with Miranda from the first time they met. Not only was she beautiful, but she was also unaware of her outward beauty. She also possessed an inward beauty which included his love for the medical profession. She treated everyone with dignity. The kind of woman he wished for to share his life. While he waited for Miranda to complete her wish, he, too, made one.

Jamming her hands into her jacket pockets, Miranda said, "Okay, star, do your thing!"

"It took so long, I'm curious as to what you wished for," Dr. Roye said.

"Didn't you just tell me it was bad luck to tell anyone your wish. That's a guarantee it won't come true," Miranda teased.

"Touché!" Dr. Roye said. "If that's the case, I won't tell you mine either."

"You made a wish?" Miranda blurted. "I thought doctors only dealt with cold, raw facts."

Still gazing skyward, Dr. Roye said, "You wouldn't believe how often I call upon the Supreme Being to guide me through difficult surgeries." After a pause, he added, "I'm *His* copilot."

Miranda was humbled. She previously had held the doctor on a pedestal. Suddenly he was human. She now felt more comfortable in his presence. Reluctantly, she said, "We better head back, otherwise Mother may send out a search party."

"Not likely!" Dr. Roye exclaimed. "She's

already treating me like a member of the family."

It's that obvious? I'm so embarrassed. At a loss for words, Miranda just turned and the two headed back the way they came.

Chapter Nine

Our Place

When it was safe to fly after the attack on Pearl Harbor, those in need of specialized treatment were transported to the States. Grady was among them. He was admitted to the Naval Medical Center in San Diego. Dr. Malcomb Gaylord, a renowned neurosurgeon, was assigned Grady's case. He ordered a battery of tests, including a CT scan to determine if Grady had a brain injury. After examining the results of the tests, Dr. Gaylord entered Grady's hospital room.

"Good morning, Petty Officer Penwell," he said, standing at the foot of the bed studying Grady's chart.

"Morning, Doc," Grady responded.

"The good news is that you don't have a brain injury," the doctor said without looking up from the chart.

"That is good news! So…what's the bad news?" Grady asked.

"Don't know if you'd call it bad news, but we haven't yet determined why you lost your memory. You appear to be healthy in every other way, so I'm sure your memory loss is temporary."

"Uh-huh. Just how long is temporary?" Grady asked.

"Another unknown," Dr. Gaylord replied. "I doubt that Freud could even answer that one."

"Where do I go from here?" Grady asked, sounding disappointed and depressed.

"Well, we think familiar surroundings may trigger your memory. As soon as we notified your parents of your diagnosis, they arranged to come take you home."

"My parents?"

"Yes. Cynthia and Wes Penwell. They're driving from Mesa, Arizona, and are scheduled to arrive today."

"Cynthia and Wes?" Grady repeated. Then after a moment, he exclaimed, "What if I don't recognize them?"

"They're aware of your situation and are prepared for any eventuality. If you don't recognize them, they'll understand. Just give yourself time to adjust and get reacquainted."

"Sure, easy for you to say," Grady mumbled.

"No, Grady, not easy for me to say. Be thankful you survived—many didn't," Dr. Gaylord scolded as he scribbled notes on Grady's chart.

Feeling foolish and ungrateful, Grady said,

"You're right, Doc. Sorry, I just…just," he couldn't finish his sentence.

There was a sudden knock on the door, but before either Grady or Dr. Gaylord could answer, the door swung open and a middle-aged couple burst into the room. The woman rushed to Grady's bedside, "Grady," she sobbed, "my baby."

Dr. Gaylord gently urged Grady's mother back onto a bedside chair. "Mrs. Penwell, I'm Dr. Gaylord, Grady's neurosurgeon."

Cynthia looked up at the doctor. "Of course, I'm sorry for my emotional outburst," she turned toward Grady's father. He was standing just inside the doorway. "This is my husband, Wes," she said. Her attention was riveted on Grady and she reached over and stroked his arm.

"Pleasure to meet you both. Grady has been the ideal patient," Dr. Gaylord said and smiled down at Grady.

Wes stepped forward and took Grady's hand. After a moment, he looked back at the doctor and asked, "Has there been any improvement?" Concern was evident in his voice.

Dr. Gaylord shook his head. "However, as we discussed during our telephone conversation, we're hopeful that relocating him to familiar surroundings will jog his memory."

Cynthia dabbed at the tears in her eyes. "We're just happy to have him back alive…"

Grady frowned, then smoothed out his expression. *These are my parents and I don't even recognize them.* He grasped his mother's hand and held it tightly, hoping for some sign of familiarity.

• • •

The next day, as soon as Grady was released from the hospital, he and his parents started the nine-hour journey back to Mesa. His father took the most scenic route hoping some landmarks might trigger Grady's memory. Grady's mother pointed out special places they visited as a family. However, much to their disappointment, nothing connected.

It was noon when they stopped at one of their favorite cafés in Yuma for lunch. As soon as they entered, they were greeted by the spicy aroma of Mexican food. Grady's father had previously researched loss of memory remedies and read that familiar odors can sometimes trigger one's memory. Growing up in Arizona, Mexican cuisine was one of the family's, and especially Grady's, favorites. He watched Grady carefully hoping to see some signs of recollection.

"Something certainly smells good!" Grady remarked. "I'm so hungry I could eat a horse."

That wasn't the reaction his father wanted, but he was still hopeful.

"Last time we stopped here, you ordered the combination plate," his mother said. "And you ate every bite!"

The threesome took a table by a window. Looking at the menu, Grady zeroed in on the combination plate. "Even though I can't remember the last time we ate here, Chimichangas, burritos, and tacos still look good to me. I'm up for an encore," he said as he closed his menu. His mother smiled.

• • •

Four hours later, as they pulled into the Penwell driveway, Grady studied the hacienda-style home with intense interest. It was tastefully landscaped. A large saguaro cactus dominated the front yard accompanied by vegetation indigenous to the area. His parents watched him rub his forehead as he struggled to remember living there.

When nothing monumental occurred, his father got out of the car and said, "Come on. Let's get inside out of this heat."

"I'll get the luggage," Grady offered, and stepped out of the car.

His mother started to protest. However, his father put a hand on her arm and shook his head.

"Your bedroom's in the same place," his father

said as they entered the house. He hoped Grady could remember where that was. Grady apparently didn't remember and looked confused. "Come on, follow me," his father finally said.

His father led him through the living area. Built in bookcases along one wall displayed a variety of kachina figures posed in various positions representing the Hopi and Zuni ritual dances. Grady stopped and studied the display. Since Grady had purchased a number of the Kachinas as gifts for his father, there was a spark of hope Grady would remember. His father stepped back to give Grady space to connect. After a few moments, without any sign of recollection, they proceeded through the living area.

"Here we are. Your room is exactly as you left it," his father said. Opening the door, he followed behind Grady.

Grady stepped inside and set his duffle on the floor. The walls were covered with pictures of Grady's academic and athletic accomplishments. He slowly approached the display and stood examining each one. His father joined him.

"That's when your team won the state basketball championship," his father said pointing to a photo of teenage boys wearing red and white basketball uniforms and broad smiles. Noticing the perplexed look on Grady's face, he added, "You were the tallest and played center. You scored twenty-six points."

"Twenty-six?"

"Yup. Your mother jumped up and down and just about did cartwheels, she was so excited."

"Ahh, Dad, I wish I could remember," Grady sighed.

He called me Dad. It was all his father could do to keep from breaking down. Faking a cough, he said, "Umm, I believe your mother made some iced tea. She's waiting for us on the patio," and he turned toward the door before the tears started.

"Wait, Dad!" Grady said. His father stopped but didn't turn back. He was unable to control the flood.

"Yes, wha…what is it?" he stuttered.

Approaching his father, Grady said, "Even if I don't regain my memory, I can tell you and Mother were the best parents a guy could ask for. Thank you."

Still with his back to Grady, all his father could do was nod. Grady opened the door and both men headed toward the patio.

"What have you two been up to…" his mother started to say but stopped when she saw the looks on their faces.

Grady took the lead. "Just a small trip down memory lane."

His mother glanced at his father. "Let me pour the tea," his father said and busied himself putting ice in the glasses.

• • •

That night after dinner, Grady lay in his bed staring at the ceiling. *Dammit! Why can't I remember anything?* was his last thought before drifting off.

• • •

Grady's father owned and operated a construction company. The morning after their return home, over breakfast, he said, "Grady, I could use some extra hands. Last week, a couple of my employees got drunk, and ended up in jail. No telling how long they'll be there."

"Sure, Dad," Grady replied. "I'd be glad to." In fact, he was relieved to have something constructive to do.

Pushing back from the table, his father said, "I have extra hard hats and gloves on site. If you're ready…"

"I'm ready," Grady answered. He stood preparing to leave when he noticed his mother standing at the kitchen sink staring out of the window. He walked up behind her, "Thanks, Mom, for the great breakfast." When she turned, he gathered her into an embrace. She couldn't suppress a sob and buried her head in

Grady's shoulder. After a moment, Grady gently disengaged and followed his father out the back door.

· · ·

Although losing his memory still haunted him, after a while, Grady acclimated and spent the next five years readjusting to his *new* life. Every so often, a word, a song, a scent, or a vision would flash across his mind but would disappear before he could connect.

His parents never gave up. One afternoon, while visiting with a neighbor, Grady's mother learned that a new clinic had opened in Phoenix. Their specialty was brain injury and memory loss restoration. Grady's mother immediately called for an appointment.

After collecting Grady's history and conducting a thorough examination, Dr. Tolson said, "I'm going to talk to your parents while you get dressed. I'll be back shortly."

Grady nodded.

Meeting with Grady's mother and father in his office, Dr. Tolson asked if there was any place in Grady's adult life that had particular or remarkable meaning.

"Hmm, I'm not sure," Grady's mother said and wrinkled her brow. After a moment of reflection, she replied, "I remember one summer before Grady left for Honolulu, he spent a couple of weeks with my sister and her husband at their place on Mallard Lake in Montana. When he came home, he wasn't the same as when he left. He then began receiving letters addressed in a female's handwriting. However, he was very private about the letters so we suspected this sender was someone special."

"Girlfriend?" Dr. Tolson asked.

"Could be," Grady's mother replied, "but I don't know for sure. We didn't intrude on his privacy."

"This is a longshot, but I think going back to, what was it? Mallard Lake?"

"Yes, near Helena, Montana," Grady's father interjected.

"Revisiting a place he may have locked in his memory may be beneficial, especially if there was emotion involved."

"I'll contact my sister and make arrangements right away," Grady's mother said, excitement evident in her voice.

"When you contact them, don't imply anything. Outside influence may initiate a false memory that doesn't exist. Grady must remember on his own," Dr. Tolson cautioned.

• • •

As soon as they arrived home, Grady's mother contacted her sister, Vivian.

"Cynthia! To what do I owe this surprise?" Vivian answered with a tinge of sarcasm in her voice.

"I know I've been lax in communication, and I apologize." After a pause, she added, "I have a favor to ask."

The tone of her sister's voice alerted Vivian something serious was coming. "You know I'd do anything for you. What is it?" Vivian replied.

"Are you planning a trip to Mallard Lake this summer?" Grady's mother asked.

A trip to Mallard Lake? "As a matter of fact, yes. Thurman is eager to do some more fishing before the season ends. Why do you ask?"

"Well, we thought we could join you. Grady always liked Mallard Lake."

"Of course! We'd love that. We planned to leave this weekend. You can come up to the lake whenever you're able. We'll meet you there," Vivian replied.

Upon receiving the invitation, Grady appeared to be excited about revisiting one of his favorite childhood haunts. They made plans to leave the next day. Grady's father put his foreman in charge of running the company for a couple of weeks, and Grady's mother packed vacation clothing for the three of them.

The drive from Mesa to Helena took two days. They arrived at Mallard Lake exhausted but excited about spending time together—and hopeful something would trigger Grady's memory. As they unloaded the car, Grady's parents watched him closely for any sign of recollection. They were disappointed that nothing unusual transpired, but they had two weeks and remained hopeful.

• • •

The three men were content to spend most days out on the lake fishing. The sisters caught up on family events and together they prepared delicious meals reminiscent of their childhood.

One day, Grady begged off the fishing trip, stating he wanted to do some hiking and exploring on his own.

"Of course," his mother said. "Lunch is at noon—"

"I'll be back by then."

As he walked along the path that encircled the lake, he came upon a weathered wooden bench. For some reason the bench seemed familiar. When he drew closer, he could see something was carved into the seat of the bench. As he examined the carving, his mind suddenly opened and he began to remember. *Miranda!* "Miranda!" he shouted. "I remember, I remember." He turned and ran back toward the cabin shouting and waving his arms above his head.

His father and uncle were fishing not far from where Grady had been walking and heard the commotion. They couldn't understand what he was saying and thinking he had been injured or bitten by a snake, they immediately rowed to shore.

Bursting into the kitchen, Grady ran to his mother. "Mother, I remember being here. The wooden bench down there," and Grady pointed to the path, "I...I remember carving our initials into the wood just before I went to Hawaii."

"That's...that's wonderful!" Grady's mother squealed as they embraced. Apparently still skeptical, she asked, "Whose initials did you carve?"

"Mine and—" before Grady could finish the sentence, his father and uncle rushed in.

"Grady!" his father shouted. "Are you alright?"

"Yes, he's just fine," Grady's mother replied, "We're just excited about Grady remembering being here."

"What! He's—"

"He was just telling us about carving some initials into the wooden bench down there when he was here before. Seeing them triggered his memory."

Grady's father looked at him. "After all these years and therapy, carved initials caused your memory to return?"

"They did, as trivial as it seems, they did," Grady responded.

"What do you remember?" his father asked.

"A beautiful girl named Miranda McClain. I remember carving our initials on the bench just as clear as if it were yesterday." Grady's face darkened. "Her mother…"

"Yes, what about her mother?" Grady's mother asked.

"She forbade Miranda from seeing me. We said our goodbyes on that bench," Grady pointed in the direction of the bench, "and vowed we'd meet again someday."

"That had to be…had to be at least five years ago," Vivian said. Then looking thoughtful, she added, "Grady's recollection is accurate. I remember Miranda McClain was here with her parents that summer. Grady would take walks around the lake with her." Vivian hung her head. "I was fearful Grady and Miranda were getting too close, if you know what I mean. I phoned Miranda's mother and told her of my concerns. As soon as she learned, she forbade Miranda from seeing Grady. That's when Grady left and went home."

Grady nodded, apparently remembering the incident as his Aunt Vivian related it. "Do they still have a place here on Mallard Lake?" he asked.

"Yes, that is as far as we know, they still own the lodge. However, I heard Rudy McClain was in poor health and we haven't seen them up here for a couple of years."

Gazing off into the distance, Grady said, "Miranda graduated in 1941. Her parents gave her a trip to Honolulu as a graduation present. I remember Agnes, her mother's sister, lived there and I met her. Miranda was there when Pearl was attacked…" Grady stopped, and looking confused, said, "Because of my injury, I lost contact and don't know what happened to her."

Suddenly all the pieces were fitting together. Grady's mother took his hand, "We can find out," she said.

"Do you really think so?" Grady whispered.

"Yes, I really think so!" his mother said emphatically.

Chapter Ten

A Wedding & A Farewell

Dr. Benjamin Roye was not only hired by Helena General but put in charge of the hospital's surgical unit. His hands-on experience during the attack on Pearl Harbor elevated him to a supervisory role. The hospital was soon touted to have the best surgical staff in the state. In fact, it became so popular, a new wing was added to accommodate the influx of patients.

Dr. Roye's expertise was reserved for the most difficult surgeries. His position gave him the latitude to request which members of his staff he wanted to help when operating. He always requested Miranda assist him.

• • •

Over the next few months, Dr. Roye and Miranda became close friends, and more.

One afternoon as they were eating lunch in the hospital's cafeteria, Dr. Roye said, "Dr. Roye is much too formal. I'd like it if you called me Ben."

"But…but what will the staff think?" Miranda protested.

Looking around the cafeteria at their coworkers,

Dr. Roye said, "Who cares?"

Miranda laughed. "Okay, Ben it is," she said and bit down on a celery stick.

• • •

Miranda and Ben spent most of their time off together, and it was soon apparent where they're relationship was headed. Miranda's mother invited Ben to dinner at least once a week.

"Mother, your actions are much too obvious—" Miranda began to chastise her mother one morning, but her mother cut her off.

"Why, what do you mean?" her mother asked. "I'm just being friendly to a stranger in our midst."

"Perhaps you haven't noticed, but Helena is, and always has been, rife with strangers. You haven't reached out to any of them. That's what I mean by being obvious."

"Nonsense! Why, I wouldn't allow any of those vagrants into our home. No telling what they would do!" her mother snapped back.

Yeah, just like the classmates you wouldn't allow me to invite to the lake. "You just made my point," Miranda said. "Anyway, I wish you wouldn't try to play matchmaker. If it's meant to be, it will be." Miranda jutted her chin defiantly. *If it weren't for Father's health, I'd get my own place! Now that I have a job, I can afford it.*

Her mother just shrugged and went back to reading the newspaper. She ignored Miranda's plea and continued to invite Dr. Roye to dinner, which appeared to be fine with Dr. Roye.

• • •

The next few months were a whirlwind. Miranda and Ben were almost inseparable. The winter gradually melted into spring and the couple would go for walks after dinner. One evening as they approached a familiar place along their path, Ben said, "Remember the evening we stopped here and made a wish?"

Miranda wrinkled her brow pretending to search her memory. "Oh, yes! Now I remember," she said. "Why do you ask?"

"I'm ready to share my wish with you," Ben said and took her hand.

"But I thought we agreed if we disclosed the wish, it wouldn't come true," Miranda protested.

"Are you willing to test the theory?"

Suddenly realizing where the conversation was headed, Miranda hesitated. "Are you?"

"I'm a risk-taker and willing to roll the dice," Ben said.

"What if they come up snake eyes?" Miranda asked.

"Hmm, the odds of rolling *losing* snake eyes

are one in thirty-six. That's not too shabby."

"Okay, you're the shooter. Go for it!" Miranda teased.

Pulling Miranda into an embrace, Ben said, "It's not complicated. I love you and want to spend my life with you. Will you marry me?"

Although Miranda suspected the proposal was forthcoming, she was still stunned. There it was right in her face. "I…I," she began.

"Just say yes!" Ben urged.

Disengaging from his embrace, Miranda turned her back to him, saying, "There's something you need to know before I answer."

Ben slumped. "Okay, I'm listening. However, nothing can change the way I feel about you."

Miranda told Ben about Grady. At the end of her narration, she said, "It's been almost five years since I last had contact with him. I don't even know if he's alive."

"Why didn't you try to find him?"

"I did. But I wasn't privy to any information because we weren't married. I couldn't ask his aunt and uncle. They would tell Mother and she'd probably lock me in my room. I hung on to the hope he would return. He knew where to find me."

"I see," Ben said. Then after a moment, added, "Don't let the past control the future. After all, it's been over for years. Do you still have strong feelings for him?"

"I'm confused and not sure," Miranda replied. "I didn't put a timeline on how long I'd wait for him. I just held out hope that he'd return. Sometimes, because of my feelings for you, I'm feeling like I'm being disloyal to Grady." Then taking Ben's hand, Miranda said, "I do love you."

Ben's sigh of relief was audible. He whispered, "Is that a yes?"

Miranda looked into his eyes, his love for her was apparent. "Yes, yes, I'll marry you."

Ben held her at arm's length and asked, "And if Grady returns?"

After a long silence, Miranda said, "I don't know how to answer that. If you're willing to take a chance…"

Pulling her close, Ben said, "I think the odds of rolling snake eyes are still one in thirty-six. I'm willing to roll the dice."

• • •

Miranda's mother was beside herself with joy. She immediately began planning the wedding. "The ceremony will be at St. Helena's Cathedral and the reception at the Montana Club. It will be the talk of the town for generations," she said to Tulla as they addressed the invitations. "Miranda's wedding dress will be a one of a kind. We're having it specially designed for her."

"Yes, ma'am," Tulla replied. She knew Miranda didn't want all of the bells and whistles but she also knew Miranda's mother was relentless.

• • •

A day before the wedding, as a surprise to Miranda, her Aunt Agnes flew to Montana to attend the wedding. Miranda's mother met her at the airport. When they arrived at the McClain residence, and as they entered the foyer, Miranda's mother called out, "Miranda, someone just delivered a wedding gift. Come see what it is."

Miranda responded, "I'll be right down." She spotted her aunt from the top of the staircase. "Aunt Agnes!" she squealed and ran down the stairs. Embracing her aunt, she asked, "How did you—"

"Your mother wanted to surprise you. It's so good to see you again, my dear."

"I missed you so much." Then turning to her mother, Miranda said, "Thanks, Mother. You couldn't have given me a more perfect wedding gift."

Her mother smiled, apparently pleased with herself for her insight. "Tulla," she said, "show Agnes to the guest room."

• • •

The day before the wedding, Miranda went to a flower shop. She was looking for roses, and asked the clerk, "What do the different colors signify?"

Pointing to the display of long-stemmed roses in the cooler, the clerk replied: "Red, of course, says love. Yellow signifies friendship; white is for peace; orange is linked to joy, and pink represents thanksgiving."

"Perfect! I'll take a white, red, and pink one," Miranda said as she extracted some bills from her wallet.

The next day, a bride couldn't have asked for a more perfect wedding day. Not a cloud in the sky as the sun smiled down on the heart of Big Sky country. As guests arrived at the church, ushers escorted them to their seats. Miranda's mother and Aunt Agnes were seated in the front row. When Tulla arrived and was ushered to a seat next to Agnes, Miranda's mother stood and bristled.

"I'm sorry, this row is reserved for *family*," she snapped.

Looking nervous, the usher pointed to the rear of the church. "I was told to escort Miss Tulla to the front row," he stammered.

"By whom?" Miranda's mother demanded.

"Mr. McClain," the usher said.

"Well, well…I never!" she said and sat back

down. *What will people think?*

Tulla was unabashed as she took her place and stared straight ahead. Agnes reached over and clasped Tulla's hand in a show of solidarity. Tulla returned the gesture.

• • •

The organist began playing Mendelssohn's *Wedding March* and all heads turned toward the entrance of the church. Miranda's father was all smiles as he proudly walked his daughter down the aisle. Before they reached the altar, Miranda pulled her father to a halt. Much to everyone's surprise, she moved along the front row where the three women were seated.

Miranda stopped in front of her mother and handed her the long-stemmed *white* rose. "Thank you for giving me life," she said. Looking surprised, her mother accepted the rose. She then stepped in front of Tulla and handed her the long-stemmed *red* rose. "Thank you for nurturing me, always being there for me, and mostly for giving me a zest for life," she said. Finally, she approached her Aunt Agnes, and handing her the *pink* rose, she said, "Thank you for sharing your home, your dreams, and your sage advice. You've been my inspiration. I'm so thankful for you." Tulla and Aunt Agnes couldn't hold back the tears. Miranda's mother remained stoic.

Rejoining her father and taking his arm, as they proceeded to the alter, her father whispered, "Nice touch." Miranda squeezed his arm in reply.

. . .

The celebrant and officiant of the wedding was Father Patrick McKenzie, a priest with an Irish brogue. The ceremony had the formality of a monarch's coronation. Miranda's maid of honor was her longtime friend, Charlotte Lancaster. Ben's best man was his brother, Darrell. Ben's side of the family was well-represented as was Miranda's. "It was a bash!" according to the newspaper account in the society section the following day.

A hush fell over the congregation when Miranda hesitated in answering when the priest asked if she took Ben as her lawfully wedded husband. Ben shifted from foot to foot as he waited. It was hard to read her expression because the veil covered her face. *Is she going to back out?* After a moment, when Miranda looked up and said in a loud, clear voice, "I do!" Ben relaxed. It was obvious the bride and groom were extremely emotional, and there wasn't a dry eye in the church by the time Father McKenzie declared, "I now pronounce you husband and wife."

It was a solemn event for both. The mutual

promises they made were not to be taken lightly and the vows were to last "until death do us part." The ceremony was picture perfect and would be forever etched in their memories and the memories of those in attendance. *It was meant to be!*

• • •

As the couple left the church, they were greeted with cheers and pelted with handfuls of rice. Miranda laughed, and ducking the deluge, she and Ben rushed to their waiting vehicle and were transported across town to the Montana Club.

The wedding feast was fit for royalty. The guests ate, drank, and made merry into the evening. Before the cutting of the cake, the traditional toasts were made. Some were poking fun at the newlyweds, but most were serious well wishes. As the toasting slowed down, all eyes turned to a couple seated near the exit when they stood. The woman wore a long-sleeved pale blue chiffon dress that covered her from her neck to her feet. Her hair was styled in an updo, reminiscent of the Gibson Girls of the 1900s. The man wore a black tailcoat suit, complete with white spats, and top hat.

An eerie hush settled over the diners when the man started to speak. "Here's to the bride and groom. We wish you a long life, prosperity, and every happiness. May all your troubles be small ones." With that he lifted his champagne glass. It was unclear what happened next, but after taking a drink it appeared the couple just disappeared. Some of the more logical minds reported they slipped away when the venue's attention was distracted when the attendees responded, "Here, here!" and joined in a drink. Others swear the couple disappeared before their very eyes. That included sober guests.

Miranda grasped Ben's arm. Ben looked at her. It was apparent she was thinking of the couple linked to the legend of Mallard Lake. "Ben, could it be?"

• • •

After the festivities, when Miranda and Ben were alone, Miranda retrieved the guest log. She ran her finger down the list, and gasped when she saw the names *Willard and Irene.*

• • •

Before the wedding, Miranda and Ben spent several weekends searching for a home. Hundreds of Victorians were built in Montana during the boom years of 1888 to 1910. Miranda had always been fascinated by the southern charm surrounding the Victorians. When their real estate agent mentioned there was an 1889 Victorian formerly belonging to Montana mining mogul, Thomas Cruse, formerly known as Thomas Cruise, for sale,

Miranda instantly wanted to see it.

When they toured the Victorian which was located across town from the McClain residence, it was love at first sight. Entering the house, Miranda exclaimed, "Oh, Ben, I love it. The Victorians and the era they represent are in some ways very romantic."

Ben raised his brow. "How can a mere house be romantic?" he questioned, as they moved from room to room in the vacant residence. Reading from a brochure, Miranda practically answered his question. "It was Thomas Cruse's gold nuggets from the Last Chance Mine that built the cathedral we were married in and it was his nuggets that built this mansion."

Ben still appeared to be skeptical, so Miranda continued by inventing a scene that would capture the romance of the era. "Close your eyes and picture it! Scarlett is sitting there on the veranda doing her tatting and Rhett has his foot on the railing smoking a cigar. 'Scarlett, you need to be kissed, and often,' he's saying to her."

Ben guffawed. "Scarlett tatting? Not likely," he snorted. "And just what did she reply?"

Looking smug, Miranda answered, "Well, 'Fiddle-de-dee', of course." She then looped her arm through his, and grinning up at him, seductively batted her eyelashes.

"You, my little vixen, are a caution, as they said back in the day. I can't deny you anything. Consider it done—the house is yours. Your very own Tara!"

Miranda squealed, hugged Ben around the neck, and then danced around in the great hall pretending to swirl imaginary skirts as she did so. Ben just laughed, reveling in Miranda's joy.

Over the next few months, the Victorian was repainted inside and out. Miranda searched the specialty shops for vintage furnishings, and by the end of the year, the house was transformed into a home reflecting the lifestyle of the Civil War era—only with modern upgrades and conveniences.

Having settled into their new home, one evening over dinner, Ben asked, "This is a pretty big house for just two people. Don't you think it's time to expand our family?"

"Whatever do you mean?" Miranda asked coyly.

"Well, I was thinking we—"

"A baby?" Miranda blurted.

Not knowing for sure if Miranda was happy or shocked by his suggestion, Ben chased an errant pea around on his plate with a fork. He didn't look up when he replied, "Yes, a baby!"

Miranda almost knocked him over when she jumped up and embraced him.

Ten months later, the couple was blessed with not only one, but two baby girls, Sandy and Mandy.

In keeping with her promise, Miranda coaxed Tulla away from her mother. Miranda's mother was taken aback that Tulla could leave her. However, she rationalized that Miranda needed help since the birth of the twins, and that was the reason Tulla left.

• • •

Miranda's father's health steadily declined. Dr. Greenwall, the family physician, made regular house calls because of Rudy's sudden onset of immobility. After one such visit, as Miranda's mother walked the doctor to the door, he whispered to her that her husband's days were numbered. He estimated Rudy had less than a month to live. Miranda's mother staggered and her hand went to her mouth to stifle a sob. The doctor took her by the elbow and gently urged her to the sofa in the living room. Once seated, she buried her face in her hands and quietly wept.

"I'm sorry to have to be the bearer of bad news," Dr. Greenwall said in a consoling tone. He placed his satchel on the floor next to the sofa and sat down beside her.

Miranda's mother waved her hand in the air. "I've…I've been expecting it, doctor," she said. "Now that it's upon us, I…I…"

The doctor nodded and reached into his bag and took out a small bottle of pills. "Here," he said. "These'll help *you* sleep." Miranda's mother robotically accepted the bottle. Realizing she was in deep thought, the doctor rose, picked up his satchel, and left the residence.

Miranda's mother stared at the bottle she held in her hand for an instant then threw it across the room. "I don't want sleep, I want my husband back!" she screamed.

• • •

It was a miserable, rainy spring day when Rudy McClain was laid to rest. After the service, family and friends gathered around the gravesite under a canopy to say their final farewells. Ben had his hands full comforting Miranda and her mother. Death was a finality. Everything Rudy accumulated during his lifetime was left behind.

Chapter Eleven

Mallard Lake

After regaining his memory and finding out what happened at Mallard Lake, Grady and his parents drove to Helena in search of Miranda. Their first stop was the newspaper. "If Miranda's parents were prominent people in Helena, major events would be big news in the society section." Addressing the clerk behind the counter, Grady's mother said, "We're looking for major social events that may have taken place as far back as four or five years ago. Do you have papers from that timeframe?"

"It would take a lot of searching to go through that many stacks of papers," the clerk replied. "What specifically are you looking for? Maybe I can help."

"Ahh, friends of ours. We lost contact with them when the war started—"

"Of course. What's their names?" the clerk asked.

"McClain."

"No kidding. I went to school with Miranda McClain. We were very close friends—"

"What's your name?" Grady interrupted.

Looking perplexed, "Charlotte Lancaster," the clerk replied.

Grady staggered and leaned against the counter. "Sir, are you alright?" Charlotte asked, her voice laced with concern.

Grady took a deep breath. "Charlotte, I'm Grady Penwell."

Now it was Charlotte's turn to gasp. "Grady, you mean *the* Grady?"

"Yes, *the* Grady."

Grady's parents stood looking on in amazement. After a moment, Grady's father glanced at his watch. Clearing his throat, he said, "Almost lunch time. Can we buy you lunch, Charlotte?"

Still stunned over the sudden realization, Charlotte nodded. "I'll let my dad know I'm going to be gone so he can cover the counter," she said.

• • •

The Cowboy Café was crowded when they entered. However, the foursome found seats at a table at the rear where it wasn't too noisy. After the waitress took their order, Grady looked at Charlotte. "You go first," he said and his voice cracked with emotion.

"Oh, Grady!" Charlotte said and reached across the table and clasped his hands.

"I'm okay, Charlotte. Just tell me what

happened."

Charlotte nodded. "After the attack, even when restrictions were lifted and she could have left, Miranda stayed in Honolulu for two reasons. One, she was waiting for your return. Two, to help her aunt, who, as you know, had a broken hip.

"Having assisted with the wounded in the hospital tents after the attack, Miranda decided she wanted to be a nurse. Since she was stuck in Honolulu, and not wanting to put off her college education for who knows how long, she enrolled in the fast-track nursing program at Paradiso University in Honolulu."

Charlotte noticed Grady was getting anxious so she truncated the rest of her story. "Long story short," she said. "When after waiting for two years, Miranda finally lost hope of ever finding you again. She had met a doctor when helping after the attack on Pearl. He was in the Navy. After serving out his enlistment, he retired from the Navy and relocated to Helena. They reconnected and were married three years ago."

After a long pause, Grady said, "Miranda's still in Helena?"

Charlotte nodded, and pointing West, said, "She lives not far from here."

Grady blanched and tears filled his eyes.

"Grady, if it's any consolation," Charlotte said, "Miranda loved you with all her heart. She still loves you… She was mystified as to why you couldn't contact her after two years if you were still alive and wondered if your feelings toward her changed."

Just then the waitress appeared with their lunches. When she retreated, Grady, now somewhat composed, said, "I was injured during the Pearl Harbor attack and have had amnesia for the last five years. One of my doctors suggested being in familiar places might help me recover my memory. The trip to Mallard Lake was hopefully to help me remember. Yesterday, up at the lake, as I walked along a path I stopped and sat down on a wooden bench near the water. When I did so I noticed someone had carved the initials GP plus MMC inside a heart on the seat of the bench. Suddenly I remembered doing that. That's when the memories came flooding in. I began to remember everything."

When Grady paused, his mother said, "That's why we showed up in Helena at the newspaper office. When Grady began to remember, we decided we'd try to find out what happened to Miranda."

"I'm sorry to have to deliver the news," Charlotte murmured. "Grady, I know how hard this must be." After a pause, she asked, "Will you try to find Miranda?"

"Don't know—" Grady started.

Charlotte interrupted, "I mean, if for no other reason than just to let her know you're still alive."

"Is she happy?" Grady asked.

"I think so. They have two-year-old twin daughters, Sandy and Mandy.

Grady nodded. "Would it be better to let sleeping dogs lie? I don't want to interfere with her life. What do you think?"

Taking a moment before answering, Charlotte finally said, "Put yourself in her place, would you want to spend the rest of your life not knowing what happened to her?"

"I see your point." Rubbing his forehead, Grady said, "Let me sleep on it. If you'll give me your phone number, I'll call you tomorrow."

Charlotte rummaged around in her purse coming up with a pen and piece of paper. She scribbled her phone number on the paper and handed it to Grady. The rest of the lunch was spent indulging in light conversation, talking about Montana and life in Arizona. It was obvious everyone's focus was on what Grady would decide to do.

• • •

That afternoon as the Penwells drove back to Mallard Lake, Grady said to his parents, "I'm in a quandary. You always gave me good advice. What should I do?"

Grady's dad shifted in his seat and positioned his elbow on the open driver's side window. Glancing at Grady in the rearview mirror, he said, "Son, these are uncharted waters. After weighing all the pros and cons, the decision is ultimately yours. My take is that Charlotte's comment about wanting to know what happened certainly hit the nail on the head. If for no other reason than to close this chapter in both of your lives, I'd want to see her."

"That's good advice, Dad. Mom, what do you think?"

"Well, Grady, mothers think with their hearts most of the time, not their minds. I don't want to see you hurt any more than is necessary. Not seeing her isn't a guarantee you won't still hurt. Dad does make a good point and I'm inclined to agree with him. You'll never know for sure, and most likely spend the rest of your life wondering if you don't take the gamble. I know if I was Miranda, I would want to hear from you." She turned around and raised her brow.

"How is it that all of a sudden you two are so smart? I remember growing up, I didn't think you knew anything."

"Yep, Cindy," Grady's father said, "your son's

beginning to sound normal." The three of them shared a much-needed laugh.

• • •

The next morning Grady called Charlotte.

"Hello," Charlotte answered the phone.

"Charlotte, it's Grady."

"Yes, Grady. I've been expecting your call," Charlotte said. "Have you made a decision whether or not to contact Miranda?"

"Yes, after discussing the pros and cons with my parents, I've decided to see her."

"You're sure?"

"Yes, why do you ask," Grady said sounding perplexed.

"What if…what if she doesn't want to see you after all this time?" Charlotte asked.

"I thought about that. If that's the case, I'll live with it and be better equipped to put her out of my mind."

"I'll phone her today and get back to you. That way it won't be such a shock. Right now, she doesn't know whether you're alive or dead."

"Thanks for still being the go-between. I owe you one—no, make that a lot."

• • •

After ending the call, Charlotte immediately phoned Miranda. "Hello," Tulla answered.

"Tulla, it's Charlotte. Is Miranda there?"

"No, Miss Charlotte. She and Dr. Ben are taking a long weekend off. They left yesterday for Yellowstone. She calls a couple of times a day from the lodge. When she calls again, is there a message?"

"No, no message. I'll contact her when they get back. Thanks, Tulla."

Charlotte immediately called Grady. "Did you talk to her?" Grady anxiously asked.

"No. Miranda and Ben are spending the weekend in Yellowstone. They left yesterday and are expected back Sunday evening. How long are you staying at Mallard?"

"I'll probably leave Monday morning. Dad's anxious about leaving his business for too long." Grady paused and wrinkled his brow. "Maybe it wasn't meant to be, Charlotte. Thanks for trying."

"You have my number if you need to contact me. It was nice meeting you and your parents."

"Same here, although I feel like I know you through my conversations with Miranda."

And I know you through Miranda's sharing your letters—wish I could find someone like you. Charlotte then asked, "Do you want me to tell—"

"No! I mean, what's the point. I wish her every happiness. You take care and God bless you."

Chapter Twelve

Serendipity

Standing in the park watching Old Faithful for the tenth time, Miranda clasped Ben's hand. "Since we've seen everything there is to see here, let's head for home. I miss the twins and if we leave early, we can go by Mallard Lake and spend the night at my folks' lodge."

"I agree. I'm eager to see this mystic lodge I've heard so much about," Ben replied.

"Don't be disappointed. It's probably dusty since no one's been there for over three or four years. Mother quit going when Father got so infirm he couldn't walk. I was thinking the lodge would be a fun place to take the girls for short getaways when they get a little older."

"Sure. Perhaps I can revive my fishing skills."

"If you do, you'll clean the fish. Yuck!"

Holding up his hands and turning them over examining them, Ben said, "These are the hands of an almost world-renowned surgeon and you want them to clean fish?"

"You catch 'em, you clean 'em. Tulla will cook 'em."

"So, Little Red Hen, I guess you'll eat 'em," Ben teased.

"Bingo! I wouldn't feel right if I didn't do my part. Come on, let's check out."

· · ·

When the couple approached the McClain lodge at Mallard Lake, Miranda became melancholy. "Gosh, nothing has changed. Mother hires a local man and his son to keep the outside vegetation trimmed. We're on our own on the inside."

Looking toward the lake, Ben exclaimed, "Beautiful setting." Then looking toward the lodge, Ben asked, "Do you have a key?"

"No, but we always kept one hidden on the outside. If you get the overnight bag, I'll get the key. Meet you at the front door."

When they entered the lodge, they were engulfed in a curtain of cobwebs. "Holy smokes!" Ben exclaimed as he pulled webs away from his face. Miranda followed close behind as they made their way into the living room.

Looking around at the mess, she muttered, "Maybe this wasn't such a good idea after all."

"Of course it was. I like it here already. Find me a broom and I'll clear a passage. What a great place to have a Halloween party…"

An hour later, after making the place livable,

Miranda opened the shopping bag she brought in. "And you, my love, have been such a good sport, I'm treating you to my specialty for dinner—peanut butter and jelly sandwiches."

"Sounds like heaven. Bring it on, I'm starved."

After dinner, when the sun was going down, Miranda and Ben sat on a wooden swing on the porch listening to the night sounds. "I could get used to this kind of life," Ben said.

"It's okay occasionally," Miranda replied. "I'm not much of a pioneer."

• • •

The next morning Miranda was up early. She stealthily slipped out of bed. Ben was sleeping so soundly, she didn't want to wake him. Quickly dressing, she went to the kitchen and found a canister of ground coffee. *Wonder if it's still good after all this time. Guess we'll find out.*

When the coffee was ready, she poured herself a cup and went outside. The sun was just coming up over the distant mountains and the scene was spectacular. Miranda set her coffee mug aside and started walking, taking in the morning freshness. Lost in nostalgia, she found herself on the path she had walked so often over the years.

• • •

When she approached the bench she and Grady

had designated as '*our* place' she thought she saw someone sitting on it. *Naw, can't be.* Getting closer, the vision became clearer and she was sure someone was there.

• • •

Realizing this would probably be the last time he would visit Mallard Lake, Grady arose early the next morning and walked to the bench he and Miranda designated as '*our* place.' *I've got to put the past behind me and get on with life.*

Grady had been sitting on the bench reliving the times he spent with Miranda. When he caught movement out of the corner of his eye, he stood. He thought he was hallucinating when he saw a figure in the distance. Then remembering the legend, he whispered, "*Irene?*" He continued to watch, and when the figure came closer it looked more like Miranda coming toward him.

"Miranda?" he said. When he said her name, she stopped.

"Grady? Is it really you?"

As soon as she spoke, Grady recognized her voice and began running toward her. Miranda did likewise. When they were only inches apart, they stopped. Miranda reached out and touched Grady's face. "You are real," she whispered.

Grady gathered her into his arms.

Miranda slumped and started to fall. As Grady held her tightly, she buried her head in his chest and sobbed tears of joy. After a few moments, Grady took her by the hand and helped her to *their* bench.

After regaining her composure somewhat, Miranda murmured, "I thought I lost you forever, what happened?"

Too emotional to immediately respond, Grady took several deep breaths before answering. "I…I was injured during the attack and lost my memory. Doctors advised revisiting familiar places could be beneficial in restoring my memory. This visit to the lake and sitting on *our* bench where I carved our initials, did the trick. Yesterday, I began to remember."

"Oh, Grady, I…I…"

"No need to explain, I know. My parents and I went to the newspaper office. Charlotte recognized me and brought me up to speed regarding what happened to you." After a pause, Grady continued, "I understand you're married and have twin daughters. I don't want to interrupt your life."

Miranda listened, tears streaming down her cheeks. "I waited and hoped for your return. Ben, my husband is a good man. I love him and couldn't hurt him…"

"And I wouldn't want you to. I'm content

knowing you're happy." Not wanting to prolong the painful encounter, he looked around and said, "You're my first real love and I'll never forget you."

"And you have a special place in my heart. I'll always love you," Miranda said. Taking his hand, she continued, "When we first met, you accused me of being influenced by romantic novels and movies."

"Yes, I remember that!"

Miranda continued, "I think one of my all-time favorite lines is from Casablanca when Rick and Ilsa parted ways. Bogie said, 'We'll always have Paris.' In our case, it's Honolulu. I'll always remember the you I knew in Honolulu."

Grady laughed at her analogy. "And I'll always remember you as the lively seventeen-year-old who had the world by the tail." Grady stood, and looking over his shoulder toward the Thornton cabin, said, "I should be getting back. We're leaving this morning."

"Me, too," Miranda said. "Take care of yourself." She stood, kissed Grady on the cheek, and walked away without saying another word.

Watching her until she disappeared around a bend, Grady suddenly felt the weight of the world was lifted from his shoulders.

Chapter Thirteen

Soaring

Months passed and the Montana winter melted into a warm, welcome spring. Charlotte often thought of Grady and wondered how he was doing. One April afternoon, as rain pelted the windows of the newspaper office, the phone rang.

"Helena Telegraph," Charlotte answered.

"Charlotte! It's Grady—"

"Grady!" Charlotte squealed.

"How have you been?" Grady asked.

"Well, and you?" Charlotte responded. She could barely hear him over the thumping of her heart.

Grady, eager to get to the reason for the call, ignored the question. "I'm on the brink of earning my pilot's license but first I must make a solo flight. It's less than two hours from here to there by air. Would you consider having dinner with me?"

Are you kidding? I'd walk on hot coals to be with you. "I would love to. Let me know your arrival time and I'll pick you up at the airport."

"Wonderful! I hoped you wound say yes, so I completed my flight plan before I called. I'll be there around five this afternoon," Grady said.

"I can hardly wait, I'm so eager to see you. We have a guest bedroom at our house. You're welcome to spend the night."

"Consider it done. See you around five."

Charlotte hung up the phone. Unable to contain her exuberance, she jumped up and shouted, "Eureka!"

Her father rushed out of his office when he heard the commotion. "What in the hell?" he said.

Charlotte rushed over and hugged him. "He's coming, Dad. He's coming—"

"Hold on, little girl. Who's coming?

"Grady, Dad. Grady's coming. He's taking me to dinner."

"Well, for havens' sake, is that what all this is about?"

Undeterred by her father's lack of enthusiasm, Charlotte said, "I invited him to use the guest room. Is that okay?"

"Of course. Since your mother died, you've been the lady of the house. Your friends are always welcome." Suddenly realizing how important this date was to Charlotte, her father said, "Take the afternoon off and do what women do to get ready."

Charlotte hugged him again, grabbed her jacket, and literally flew from the newspaper office.

Her father watched through the window as she

headed up the street. *Ahh, to be young again.* Back at his desk, he made a call to their housekeeper. "Elsie, this is Lloyd. Would you be available to spruce up the house a bit this afternoon? We have a very important guest spending the night."

• • •

The trip to the beauty salon and then the boutique to purchase a *smashing* new dress took most of the afternoon. Standing in her room, after she dressed for the occasion, Charlotte examined herself in the full-length mirror.

"Charlotte, you look like a princess," Elsie said.

"Oh, thank you. This date is probably the most important event in my life."

"Hmm, hope he's worth it," Elsie said, then continued vacuuming.

Oh, he is. He certainly is!

Charlotte was waiting in the terminal when Grady landed. When she saw him coming across the tarmac, her heart raced.

As soon as he saw her, he waved. Entering the terminal, he immediately went into an office. Charlotte could see him through the open-door conversing with an airport official. At the end of their conversation, both men nodded and shook hands. When Grady came out, he walked up to her.

Approaching Charlotte, Grady said, "Filing

my flight plan for tomorrow's return trip." Then stepping back, he set his duffel down and took both of her hands in his. Admiring her, he maneuvered her into a pirouette to get a 360 view, and said, "My, you look fabulous!"

Charlotte blushed. "Thank you, so nice to see you again," she said. "I'm parked right out front," and she pointed to the front entrance.

Grady stored his duffel in the trunk, and as Charlotte cleared the parking lot, he asked, "Where would you like to eat?"

"Depends. What sounds good to you?"

"I've been doing some research on your fair state. Since Montana's a cattle capital, and you have millions of cows statewide, I was thinking about a nice, juicy steak," Grady said.

"Luca's is a nice steak house and it's close by."

• • •

The couple appeared to be comfortable in each other's company. After placing their order, nervously twisting a spoon around in his fingers, Grady said, "I saw Miranda up at Mallard Lake."
"Oh, what happened?"

"The long and short of it is that we both agreed to let the past stay in the past," Grady responded.

Maybe I do have a chance. Charlotte asked, "Is that all?"

"We parted friends. I think we're both ready to move on."

They remained silent. When dinner was served, hoping to redirect Grady's attention, Charlotte asked, "What made you take up flying?"

"Ahh, good question. When I was stationed at Pearl, the *Arrow* was moored close to where we could see the carriers, and I could see the planes take off and land on the decks. It was fascinating. I don't know when I caught the 'flying bug' but it's been nagging me for a long time, so I finally took the plunge. After an extensive ground school education, I was allowed to go up and take the controls with a supervisor with me. That was the thrill of a lifetime. It's been my passion ever since, and I hope someday to buy a plane of my own."

Charlotte sat transfixed. When Grady paused, she said "I've never flown—"

"What! Well, we can take care of that! That is, if you want to," Grady said and took a bite of sirloin, while he waited for an answer.

Charlotte fidgeted with her fork for a moment. "You mean you would take me up?" she asked.

"Damn betcha! It would be my honor."

"When?"

"Tomorrow."

"You're on," Charlotte said with a broad smile.

• • •

After dinner, when they arrived at the Lancaster residence, they paused on the front porch while Charlotte unlocked the door. Five years ago, she had suspended the wind chime Miranda brought her from Hawaii on one of the eaves on the porch. When it chimed in the slight breeze, Grady looked up. "I remember buying two windchimes when Miranda was in Hawaii. One for her and one for you. Is that the same one?"

Charlotte looked at the chime. "Yes, it's been there ever since Miranda gave it to me," she replied and opened the door.

The house was silent when they entered. "Dad is usually up at 4:00 to get the newspapers ready for delivery. He almost always goes to bed early." Setting her purse on the table in the entrance way, she continued, "You must be tired, I'll show you the guest room."

"Thank you, I am pretty beat. I was up early, too. Besides, I want to be fresh when we take you on your 'maiden voyage' tomorrow."

• • •

Charlotte's father had already left by the time Grady arose. The aroma of bacon beckoned to him and he dressed and wandered into the kitchen.

"Good morning," he said when he saw Charlotte

standing at the range.

"Well, good morning to you, too." Holding up a spatula, she said, "How do you like your eggs?"

Grady walked up behind her and snagged a strip of bacon from the serving dish. She playfully swatted at his hand and then pointed to the table which was set for two. "Sit down and I'll pour you a cup of coffee."

"I take my eggs any way they turn out. An egg is an egg by any other name. My over easy ones usually end up being scrambled," Grady said as he munched on the pilfered strip of bacon.

Charlotte poured coffee and then brought two plates to the table and sat down on the opposite side.

Eying the breakfast, Grady exclaimed, "Perfect!"

Charlotte blushed. No one had ever accused her of doing anything perfectly. "When do you want to leave?" Charlotte asked.

"Leave?"

"Oh, not for home, I mean for the maiden voyage," Charlotte said.

"Ahh, thought you were trying to get rid of me. As soon as we get the dishes cleaned up. My mother, and the Navy, trained me well."

• • •

The airport was buzzing with activity when the couple arrived. "Wait here," Grady said. "I'll check to make sure we're cleared for takeoff." A few minutes later, he reappeared and took her hand. When he took her hand, he noticed she was trembling. "We're good to go. Are you alright?"

"Yes, I'm just excited," Charlotte said. She felt warm and comfortable with Grady and trusted him with her life, literally.

• • •

When they were airborne, Charlotte couldn't take her eyes off the view. They flew over Helena and she squealed as she recognized familiar sights, pointing them out to Grady. The most impressive was the Cathedral of Saint Helena with its pointed spirals jutting skyward. Seeing it from the air as well as the Sleeping Giant Mountain gave her a whole new perspective. *Wonder if this is how God sees us?*

"So, what do you think?" Grady asked.

"I'm...I'm speechless," Charlotte replied and slipped her arm through his, hugging it tightly.

After landing, Grady said, "I'm going to leave as soon as I see you to your car."

"Oh, you don't have to do that," Charlotte protested.

"Leave or see you to your car?" Grady joked.

"Both!" Charlotte countered.

"Oh, but I do. Mother taught me to always be a gentleman and see a lady to her car. If I disobey, I'll get a whipping."

"Okay then, Red Baron, I don't want to be the cause of you getting punished."

As they walked to Charlotte's car, she asked, "When will I see you again?"

"When do you want to?"

Taken by surprise, Charlotte wanted to say, "Now and forever." However, she answered, "As often as possible."

"That can be arranged since I'm only two hours away."

When they reached her car, Grady took her in his arms and kissed her gently. Having had her feelings for him pent up for so long, she embraced him tightly and returned the kiss with passion.

"Wow, we need to go flying more often."

Embarrassed by her boldness, Charlotte blushed, opened the car door, and slid onto the car seat. Grady closed the door, and leaning forward, placed his hands on the ledge of the open window, asking, "What are you doing next weekend?"

The surprised look on Charlotte's face was unmistakable. "Ahh," she began. Then it hit her. *Oh, my God!* "If I'm lucky, I'll be flying with a very special guy."

"Consider yourself lucky!" Grady stepped back. "Until then."

"Yes, until then." *And I can hardly wait!* Afraid she'd make a fool of herself if she hung around much longer, she put the car in gear and sped off.

He watched until he could no longer see her and then, whistling, went back into the terminal.

Chapter Fourteen

Big Sky Country

The next week Charlotte appeared to be on cloud nine. Her father noticed she could hardly keep her mind on her work. She hummed as she went about her duties and he would catch her staring out of the window, lost in thought. One afternoon, she returned from lunch carrying several bags from the Last Chance Gulch department store—something totally out of character for her. *Is this my little girl?*

Charlotte was twenty-three and it appeared Cupid's arrow finally pierced her heart. Her father couldn't have been happier for her. *It's about time.* Although, during his last visit to Helena, Grady had spent the night at the Lancaster residence, her father missed meeting him because of having to be at the newspaper office so early. He was now eager to meet the young man who perpetrated this change in his daughter.

• • •

After waiting an eternity, it was finally Friday. She was eagerly awaiting a call from Grady advising her of his time of arrival the next day, Charlotte grabbed the phone each time it rang, hoping it would be him.

"Helena Telegraph," Charlotte answered for the umpteenth time.

"Charlotte, it's Grady."

Finally, the much-awaited call came and Charlotte breathed a sigh of relief. *It wasn't just a fantasy.*

"Grady! Are you still coming?" Charlotte asked and held her breath.

"Damn straight! However, it looks like a storm is moving in so I'm leaving this afternoon rather than tomorrow morning."

Eurika! "What's your ETA?"

"Whoa! You're beginning to sound like traffic control. I like women who talk my language."

Charlotte giggled. "Three abbreviated words hardly equals an entire dialect…but I'm working on it."

"That's my girl," Grady said. "My ETA is 6:00 p.m. That work for you?"

My girl. He called me 'my girl. "Damn straight! I'll be there to pick you up."

Grady smiled. "Easy on the language. Some of it is Gradyisms," he said. Then looking at his watch, he said, "Gotta run. Looking forward to seeing you. 'Til then."

"'Til then," Charlotte responded. "Don't pick

up any hitchhikers!"

Charlotte gently replaced the phone in its cradle. However, she kept her hand on the receiver. It was as though she was reluctant to break the connection with Grady.

"Everything alright?" her father asked, approaching the counter.

"Yes, Dad. Everything is just perfect!"

Her father smiled. "You want to take the afternoon off?"

"If you don't mind. I was toying with the idea of fixing dinner for the three of us. That way you can meet Grady…"

"Well, then, get yourself on outta here and get ta cookin'," her father joked. "Your mother's apple pie recipe is always a hit."

"Don't be so subtle, I can take a hint."

"Hint, hell. That was an outright request. You know what they say, 'The way to a man's heart is through his stomach!'"

Charlotte rolled her eyes and headed for the door. Before the door shut completely, she called to her father, "I love you, Dad. You'll always be my number one."

If he was physically able, her father would have jumped up and clicked his heels together. His heart was so full of joy for his daughter.

* * *

Charlotte was waiting at the airport when Grady landed. Eager to greet him, she went to the entrance when she saw him coming across the tarmac. As soon as Grady stepped into the terminal, he dropped his duffel and pulled Charlotte into a welcoming embrace.

"Hello, beautiful," he said. "It's nice to see you again."

"And I you," was all Charlotte could manage for fear she would start to cry and spoil the evening.

After clearing with the airport officials, the couple headed for Charlott's car.

"Good thing I came early," Grady said. Then looking skyward, he said, "Tony told me the incoming storm appears to be getting pretty violent. They may close the airport until it passes." Then taking her hand, Grady said, "That's not the only reason I'm glad I came early."

Not wanting to get sentimental for fear she'd reveal too much of her feelings, Charlotte said, "I hope you like apple pie…"

"What! You're kidding. I don't like it, I love it!"

* * *

When they left the terminal, the wind had picked up and it had started raining. Holding her purse to the top of her head to keep her hair dry,

Charlotte shouted, "Follow me." The couple ran, splashing through puddles that were now forming, to Charlotte's car.

Once safely inside the vehicle, Grady said, "Looks like this is going to be a doozy. Hopefully, it will pass by the time I have to leave on Sunday."

"If not, you're welcome to stay as long as need be," Charlotte said. *How 'bout forever?*

• • •

Thankfully, the Lancasters had a carport close to their covered front entrance. When Charlotte pulled up under the canopy, Grady jumped out, retrieved his duffle, and rushed to join Charlotte who was already on the porch.

When they entered the living room, Charlotte's father was resting in his easy chair. He immediately rose and extended his hand to Grady.

"Dad, I want you to meet Grady Penwell," Charlotte said and the pride in her voice was unmistakable.

"Well, young man, it's about time we met. You've had Charlotte in a twitter for weeks."

Charlotte groaned. "Dad!" she blurted.

"What? Did I say something wrong?"

Grady to the rescue. "No, sir, Mr. Lancaster. You did just fine," he said, and winked at Charlotte who had turned a deep shade of red.

Turning toward the kitchen, Charlotte finally managed to say, "I'll go check on dinner." As she left the room, she added, "Since the cat's already out of the bag, you two may as well go ahead and get acquainted."

Charlotte's dad sat back down and pointed to the sofa. "Take a seat, Grady." Then rubbing his brow with his fingertips, he added, "Guess I'll never understand women."

"You're not alone, Mr. Lancaster. There's about a bazillion males out there who feel the same way, including me."

Charlotte's dad chuckled. "Call me Lloyd."

The two men engaged in conversation, mostly sports, until Charlotte announced dinner was ready. When they gathered around the dining room table, Charlotte's dad asked Grady to say grace. He always asked their guests to say grace. This was his secret way of determining if their guests were Christian. Grady did the honors.

The dinner conversation was centered on news of the day and sports. Being in the newspaper business, the Lancasters were knowledgeable on current events. Grady was surprised to learn that Charlotte liked football and was a Cleveland Browns fan.

"Thought you'd lean toward the Giants,"

Grady said, as he popped the last bite of roast into his mouth.

"The Giants are a good team, as well as the Bears. However, Cleveland is rated number one this season. I like winners!"

Grady placed his napkin on the table and set his fork on his plate. Looking at Charlotte, he said, "Best pot roast I've ever had—but don't tell my mom."

"Why, thank you," Charlotte responded as she rose. Collecting the dishes, she asked, "Did you save room for apple pie?"

"Indeed, I did. I've been anticipating it ever since we arrived."

Charlotte raised her brow. "How'd you know?" she asked.

"Smelled it when we entered the house."

Charlotte nodded and went into the kitchen. She returned with three pieces of apple pie.

When the diners finished their pie, Grady reached across the table and took Charlotte's hand. "At the risk of sounding like a parrot, I must say that was the best apple pie I've ever eaten—"

"I know… but don't tell your mom," Charlotte said and stood. "You two go on. I'll—"

"Oh, no you don't. You cook, I clean," Grady interrupted, and reached over and untied the apron

Charlotte was wearing, and pulling it off, tied it around his waist.

Placing her hands on her hips in a defiant manner, Charlotte said, "Fifty-fifty, or no deal. I wash, you dry."

"I can do that," Grady smiled.

"Dad, you go relax."

"You sound like a drill sergeant," Charlotte's father said as he left the dining room. However, inside he was bubbling over with joy. *I like that young man.*

· · ·

The rain moved out overnight. The next morning, when Charlotte's dad arose and began puttering around preparing a pot of coffee, the phone rang.

"Hello," he answered.

"Lloyd, it's Frank. We have an emergency situation!"

Instantly alerted, Charlotte's dad asked, "What's that?"

"Lightning started a forest fire just outside of town. I just found out Jack Loring had taken a Boy Scott troop into that forest near Mallard Lake. We think they're stranded on the other side of the fire. Our only hope is to try to find them from the air since no one can get in from this side."

"Have you notified the—"

"All of the emergency responders are tied up at the lake fighting the fire."

Just then Charlotte and Grady entered the kitchen. "What's going on?" Charlotte whispered.

Her father covered the mouthpiece. "Lightning started a forest fire up at the lake. Jack and a troop of scouts are stranded on the other side of the fire. Frank said the fire is so big, the only way to locate them is from the air."

"Okay…what's the problem?"

"All the responders are fighting the fire. There are no pilots available to do a flyover."

"Yes, there is," Grady interjected. "Tell them I'm on my way. Have someone meet me at the airport to give me the coordinates."

"You're not going alone," Charlotte said. "I'm going with you."

"I don't think that's a good—"

"We don't have time to argue about it. Let's go."

Charlotte's dad was back on the phone as he watched the couple back out of the driveway. "Frank, Charlotte's friend—"

"I overheard. I'm on it."

• • •

When Charlotte and Grady arrived at the airport, they were met by an envoy and ushered into an office where a map was spread on a desk. Tony, the airport manager, took charge of the briefing. He circled the area where the fire was raging. Then pointing to the opposite side of Mallard Lake, he said, "This is where we believe the scouts are stranded. However, we have no way of knowing for sure and it's too dangerous to send a crew in to search."

"I'm somewhat familiar with the lake," Grady said. "I think I know the vicinity you think the scouts may be in."

"The fire is moving so rapidly, we need to get going," Tony said. "We think we can get a helicopter in if we can get them to a clearing wide enough for a chopper to set down."

"Let's go!" Grady exclaimed.

Running toward Grady's plane, Tony said, "We refueled your plane yesterday after you left so it should be ready."

Grady hadn't noticed Charlotte keeping pace behind them. When they approached his plane, she shouted, "I'm going with you!"

Grady was already climbing into the cockpit. He snapped, "No! It's too dangerous."

Charlotte, right behind him, already had one leg in the plane. "You need another pair of eyes. I'm very familiar with the lake and can help…"

"Oh, for Pete's sake! Come on," he said.

As Charlotte was getting situated, he started the engine and revved it up. Quickly checking the instruments, he stuck his hand out of the window and gave Tony a thumbs up.

Tony backed away from the plane and saluted Grady. "May God be with you," he shouted over the din of the engine. A minute later the plane was airborne.

Chapter Fifteen

Rescue Mission

Jack Loring knew as soon as the fire was reported, a search and rescue team would be deployed. He was savvy enough to realize the only way they could be rescued was by helicopter. When it was obvious that the fire was getting closer to the scouts' location, Jack gathered the fifteen teens around him. "Collect your gear and prepare to move to the clearing on the other side of the trees."

The smoke was getting thick and it was becoming difficult to breathe. They could hear trees exploding in the distance. "Mr. Loring," fourteen-year-old Sammy Turner asked in a trembling voice, "are we going to be alright?"

Jack glanced at the other teens gathered behind Sammy. They all appeared to be apprehensive and impatient as they awaited a response. "Yes, we are," Jack said loud enough for everyone to hear. "I'm sure a team is on the way to rescue us. Our job is to stay calm."

"What if they can't find us?" asked another member of the troupe.

"Search and rescue," Jack began, "are aware

of our exact location and are familiar with the terrain. I'm sure a rescue was instituted as soon as the fire was reported. That's what they're trained to do." Jack paused, "In the meantime, we need to do our job."

Jack looked for the most likely site for a helicopter to land. One that was a safe distance away from the heart of the fire. It was covered with debris that might interfere with the landing. Although it was as hot as an oven where they stood, and sparks were flying overhead, Jack instructed the boys to clear as much as they could. Keeping them busy also served a psychological purpose—to minimize panic.

It was late afternoon by the time the makeshift landing pad was cleared. Jack knew the boys were hungry although no one complained. To distract them and keep them calm, he instructed the scouts to sit in a circle and eat the MREs they brought with them.

When they were finished with their meal, in true kumbaya spirit, Jack began to lead them in hymns. *Now all we can do is wait—and pray,* he thought.

• • •

The trip by air from Helena to where the fire was raging took less than twenty minutes. Grady's attention was solely on the instruments displaying the coordinates he received at the airport. Charlotte strained her eyes as she looked down into the fire for any sign of the scouts.

"Anything?" Grady would occasionally ask.

"Not yet," Charlotte would reply.

After a few minutes of unsuccessful searching, Charlotte suggested they try the other side of the lake.

"That's not within the perimeter of the coordinates," Grady said.

"But we haven't seen anything in the designated section. Jack may've moved them," Charlotte argued.

"Okay, what've we got to lose."

As soon as they crossed to the opposite side of the lake, Charlotte pointed. "Look," she said, "there's a beam of flickering light. That must be a signal from Jack indicating their location."

Grady immediately turned the plane in the direction of the light. When the scouts heard the engine of the plane. They all jumped up and started waving their arms in the air.

Charlotte shouted. "You found them."

"Praise God," Grady whispered, then added, "*You* found them." He then took her hand, "I'm glad you came along. I need a guardian angel." He proceeded to report their location via radio to the airport. "We found them and there's a spot for a helicopter to land."

· · ·

Tony had been standing by waiting for the call. "Good work! Give me the coordinates and I'll dispatch the chopper right away."

Before leaving the area, Grady flew low over the site and dipped his wings, indicating they were spotted and that help was on its way. He and Charlotte watched the boys as they excitedly jumped up and down, waving recognition.

· · ·

The rescue was executed without a hitch. As they gathered in the terminal at the airport, Jack approached Grady. "The smoke was so thick, it was a miracle that you found us."

"Not a miracle, that beam of light you flashed led us directly to you."

"Beam of light?"

"Yes, didn't you—"

"No, we didn't."

Grady looked at Charlotte. She just shrugged. *Willard and Irene*?

· · ·

EVERYDAY HEROES, was the newspaper headline the following day. The story depicted in explicit detail the daring and successful rescue of the scouts. Grady Penwell was instantly thrust into the limelight.

"Too bad you're not a Montana resident," Charlotte's father said over dinner.

"Why's that?" Grady asked.

Without taking his eyes from his plate, Charlotte's father said, "You'd be a shoo in for governor."

"Governor? I don't have a political background—"

"Don't need one to figure out right from wrong. You have a good head on your shoulders. Think about it. You're a veteran and now a heralded local hero. We need good, honest representatives at the helm. Those who won't pander to the powerful or be swayed by public opinion." Smearing butter on a roll, Charlotte's father continued, "You just need to establish a year's residency and then the world is your oyster."

• • •

That evening sitting on the porch with Charlotte, Grady asked, "You think your father was serious about the governor comment?"

"Dad doesn't toy around. He calls 'em like he sees 'em. So, to answer your question, yes, I believe so."

After a pause, Grady asked, "What do you think?"

"I'm my father's daughter. No sugar coating from me. Here's my take. I think you'd be a great governor. However, you may want to consider running for state representative or the senate before jumping right into the governorship."

Grady remained silent for so long, Charlotte was afraid he had fallen asleep. "Grady? Are you alright?"

"Yes, just thinking."

Grady walked to the railing that surrounded the porch and leaned against it facing Charlotte. Even though it was twilight, he could still make out her features. She looked up at him when he finally said, "Although we've only personally known each other for a short time, I feel like I know you quite well through Miranda's eyes. I've grown to respect you and…love you. What would you say to becoming the wife of the next future governor?"

Charlotte suddenly became light-headed. *Did I hear that right?* Grady waited a few agonizing moments for an answer. When she was finally able to speak, she said, "Are you asking me to marry you?"

Grady whispered, "Yes, yes, I am. Maybe it's too soon—"

"Oh, no you don't!" Charlotte squealed. "Yes! I'd love to be the future governor's wife."

Immediately joining Charlotte on the swing, Grady embraced her and felt tears on her cheeks as they sealed the deal with a kiss.

Charlotte's father just happened to be sitting by an open window and overheard the whole exchange. *Eurika!* he thought and silently slipped into his bedroom unnoticed.

• • •

The next morning when Charlotte and Grady announced their engagement to Charlotte's father, he said, "Congratulations! I'd be honored to have you as a son-in-law. You need to establish residency as soon as possible," he said. "If you can delay your return to Arizona until Monday, you can apply for a Montana driver's license. All you have to do is show identification and your intent to become a citizen of Montana. I'm not sure what the waiting period is."

Charlotte looked suspiciously at her father. His reaction was not one of surprise, and it was apparent he'd been thinking about the process of establishing residency. Suddenly, it was obvious to Charlotte that her father knew about the engagement before they told him.

"You ol' coot! You've been eavesdropping."

Charlotte's father laughed. "It's in my genes. Good reporters always get the scoop first."

Grady had been observing the exchange as he sat in the breakfast nook drinking coffee. "Well, now that it's official, we need to call my parents," he said.

"Indeed, you do. And right away!" Charlotte's father insisted.

Grady's mother answered the phone on the first ring. When Grady told her of the engagement, she shouted, "Wes! Wes, come in here. Grady and Charlotte are engaged to be married."

Grady could hear his father in the background. "What, what's this?" he demanded.

"Grady and Charlotte are going to get married."

"Well, I'll be…" was all his father could say.

• • •

After her father left for the newspaper office, Charlotte sat down next to Grady. She seemed to be preoccupied as she stirred her coffee.

"Is something bothering you?" Grady asked.

"No, why?"

"Since you don't use cream or sugar, I'm just wondering what you're so intent on stirring. You've almost stirred a hole in the bottom of that cup. What's up?"

Charlotte immediately set her spoon aside. "Well, there is one thing," she began.

"Okay, I'm listening," Grady said looking into

her eyes for any sign of what the problem could be.

"As you already know," Charlotte began, "Miranda has been my best friend for many years. I would like for her to be my maid of honor at our wedding—"

"Is that all!" Grady blurted. Taking Charlotte's hand, he pressed it to his lips and tenderly kissed it before continuing, "I have no problem with that whatsoever. Miranda was a big part of my life— *was* is the operative word here. After meeting with her at the lake, I think we're both over the *first love* infatuation syndrome. *You* are now my life. I'm older and much wiser, well, I hope much wiser. I don't want to start our journey together with any doubt dangling over your head. I don't know how else I can say it, and I hope you'll believe it, but I love *you* and only *you*, now and forever."

"Oh, Grady, I…I…," Charlotte paused and pressed a fist against her lips stifling a sob. Grady sat, holding her other hand, silently waiting. When Charlotte was back in control of her emotions, she continued. "I…I fell in love with you through Miranda's reading me your letters. You spoiled me. No other boy even came close to my vision of you. *You* are my life and I can hardly believe you want to spend your life with me."

"I'd be a fool to let you slip through my fingers."

Putting his arm around her shoulders, he pulled her close. "Never doubt my love for you. I couldn't bear losing you."

"And I you," Charlotte replied.

"Now that that's settled, I'm leaving the wedding plans up to you. Whatever you want…"

"Whatever I want?"

"Well, within reason, no drunken brawls! Remember, if your dad's prediction proves to be correct, we may be living in the White House in the future so keep the skeletons out of our closet!"

"Holy smokes, the White House? Squeaky clean, I promise," Charolette said.

• • •

Charlotte's father insisted Grady move in with them immediately. "You can't take the time to look for houses. Grady must establish residency for at least a year to run for office. The next election is barely a year away."

"But—" Charlotte began to protest.

"But nothing!" her father snapped. "There's not a single argument you can bring that would make sense. After the wedding, you two will have time to look for a place. But right now, time is of the essence. Case closed!"

• • •

Taking Charlotte's father's sage advice, Grady

moved in with the Lancasters. Tony, the airport manager, had watched Grady as Grady flew in and out of Helena. He was impressed with Grady's skill, as well as his having participated in the rescue of the scout troop. When Tony learned Grady was relocating to Helena, he pulled him aside one afternoon.

"Come on into my office," Tony said. "There's something I want to talk to you about."

"Sure, Tony. Is there something wrong?"

"What? Oh, hell no! Nothing like that." After they were seated, Tony crossed his arms and leaned back in his leather chair. "I'm getting up there in years," he said. "I'd like to take a day off once in a while, but I don't have anyone on the payroll I feel comfortable leaving in charge here."

"Okay," Grady said, wondering why Tony was confiding in him.

"You're the kind of guy I want on my team. I'm offering you the position of assistant manager of the airport."

A stunned Grady just stared at Tony. Tony laughed, "You look like the proverbial deer in the headlights," he said.

"Ahh, your offer was so unexpected… I don't know what to say."

"Take some time to think about it," Tony

suggested.

"Don't need time," Grady replied. "I like it but I don't have any experience in managing."

"You don't need experience. You're educated and have good common sense. Experience comes with participation. You're a quick learner."

"Well, okay then," Grady said with a broad smile. "When do I start?"

"Whenever you're ready," Tony said and stood extending his hand to Grady. They shook closing the deal.

Grady's life was changing so rapidly in a positive way, he could hardly believe it. His head was spinning. Although Grady missed his parents, he was grateful to have the stability of living at the Lancasters, rather than solo in an unfamiliar environment. Most evenings, after dinner, they would sit in the living room or when the weather permitted, the front porch. Grady soon learned that Charlotte loved the rain. The two men in her life indulged her and would sit on the porch watching it rain and discussing everything from politics to religion.

These evening sessions were beneficial to Grady. He became acquainted with his new surroundings through the conversations with the Lancasters. Charlotte's father had his finger on the pulse of the county, not to mention the state. "In the newspaper business," he said, "it pays to know what's going on and how it affects you. It is also a way to attract public opinion and identify the issues.

Chapter Sixteen

Déjà Vu

Three months after their engagement, Grady and Charlotte were married at St. Helena's Cathedral. Miranda was Charlotte's matron of honor, and Tony was Grady's best man. The wedding was the social event of the season and the cathedral was packed.

Charlotte was straight out of a fairytale in her antebellum-style wedding gown and Grady eventually cowboyed up and agreed to wear the "monkey suit." Although uncomfortable, he was movie-star handsome in his tuxedo. However, Miranda and Ben's three-year-old twins, Sandy and Mandy, stole the show. Dressed in pale pink versions of the wedding gown, they preceded Charlette and her father up the aisle carrying small white wicker baskets of pink roses. They stopped periodically and handed a rose to whoever was seated at the end of the pew—male or female, it didn't matter. The girls beamed and seemed to delight in the abundance of attention they received.

"Thought this was *your* wedding," Charlotte's father whispered as they trailed along behind the twins.

Charlotte was so happy, she ignored the insinuation and just giggled at her father's comment.

• • •

After the wedding ceremony, a reception was held at the Montana Club. The guests, having indulged in several glasses of champagne, were jovial and boisterous. Adhering to the tradition of toasting the newlyweds, friends and relatives began to take turns toasting.

Suddenly Miranda remembered the odd couple who showed up at her wedding. Seated at the head table, she began to scan the guests looking for who she thought could be Willard and Irene. She relaxed when she determined everything appeared to be normal. However, before the toasting was completed, all heads turned toward the rear of the reception room when someone rapped a knife against a glass to get their attention. They were looking at the same couple who appeared at Miranda's wedding—dressed just as they had been at Miranda's wedding. Miranda remembered that the woman wore a long-sleeved pale blue chiffon dress that covered her from her neck to her high-topped buttoned shoes. Her hair was still styled in an 1890s updo. The man wore the same type of black tailcoat suit, complete with white spats, and top hat.

Déjà vu gripped Miranda when the man started to speak, she remembered his voice from her wedding.

"Here's to the bride and groom. We wish you a long life, prosperity, and every happiness. May all your troubles be small ones. May you always be guided by the beam of light that beckons from beyond." With that he lifted his champagne glass, and just as before, the couple disappeared right before the attendees' eyes.

Charlotte grabbed Grady's hand. "Grady, that was Willard and Irene, you know, the couple told about in the Mallard Lake legend. They must've been the one's that provided the beacon of light we followed when the scouts were spotted and rescued."

Grady shook his head, not so much in disagreement but to clear it. "I've never believed in spirits, but…"

Chapter Seventeen

The Candidate

The newlyweds settled into their new lives. Their first order of business was to find a home. Because of his new job, Grady spent most of his time at the airport. However, working for her father, Charlotte's job provided her the latitude to hunt for a house.

One morning before leaving for work, Grady said, "We can save time by doing several things at once. You're familiar with the city, which is important in selecting a permanent place to live. If you agree, you can do the leg work and look for a home for us. I'll be happy with whatever you decide, that is provided we can afford it. However, I'd like to see it before you sign on the dotted line." "Good idea," Charlotte agreed. The thought of having her own home thrilled her. "I'll get started on it today."

"Okay but remember the 'provided we can afford it' clause in our agreement!" Grady cautioned.

Charlotte just rolled her eyes.

• • •

When Grady's parents learned that their son was going to run for the Montana House of

Representatives, they contributed generously to his campaign fund.

"Dad, I can't accept this. I'm not even running in Arizona," Grady protested when his father handed him a check.

"Yes, you can. Your mother and I earmarked a savings account for your college education. Since you didn't go to college, the money is still yours. Besides, which state doesn't matter when it comes to effective governance. The laws enacted affect the whole country, not just the individual states. Our country needs strong, Christian, confident leaders bent on doing the right thing for the union, not just to line their own pockets. The whole is only as good as the sum of its parts."

Grady embraced his father. "Thanks, Dad. I'll try to make you proud of me."

"You've already done that by just being the person you turned out to be. Everything else is icing on the cake!"

• • •

Charlotte's father, being experienced in designing and printing political ads, took over getting the message out to the public that Grady was running for the recently vacated Montana House of Representative's seat. He was in his element and savored having had a hand in encouraging his son-in-law to pursue a political career. Charlotte even noticed his enthusiasm as he labored over composing, typesetting, and laying out the photography for the ads for Grady's presentation.

Grady insisted he pay the going price for the advertisements. He didn't want any skeletons to come back to haunt them.

Charlotte's father guffawed. "Well, that's a switch, an honest politician. Hang on to your principles, Grady, no matter what the cost!" he cautioned.

· · ·

As the summer turned into fall, *Dignity and Opportunity for All!* became a war cry. Charlotte's father had media connections throughout the state and soon after his announcement, Grady was known statewide—Grady Penwell became a household name. The citizens of Montana, and especially those in Helena, gave generously to his war chest. Top newscasters clamored to do interviews with him—including multiple television appearances.

Grady's all-American boy good looks swayed the females and his take-charge attitude swayed the males. Being a veteran and helping rescue the Scouts added flavor to his resume. His campaign slogan, *Dignity and Opportunity for All!* caught on like wildfire. Charlotte's father had campaign buttons made and distributed them throughout the state. The opposition was taking a beating and it looked like Grady would be a shoo-in.

• • •

Somehow, through all the hoopla, Charlotte found the house of their dreams; one that Grady approved of after a cursory inspection. Grady was spread so thin between his job and campaigning, family and friends pitched in and helped Charlotte obtain furniture and the necessities to get settled in their new home. After the last picture was hung, a crew of housewives showed up with mops and dust clothes. The place was spotless when they left.

As preplanned, Charlotte met Grady at her father's house and took him to their new home. She had previously had a campaign poster positioned on their front lawn. When they pulled into the driveway, pointing at the poster, Grady said, "Nice touch! I like this place already."

"I thought you would," Charlotte said. She then made him close his eyes, and taking his hand, led him inside.

"Don't peek," she scolded.

"Wouldn't do it," Grady said as he stumbled along the driveway.

After closing the front door behind them, Charlotte said, "Okay, open your eyes."

It took Grady a moment to adjust to the light. When he could finally see clearly, he shouted, "Eureka! I don't just like it, I love it!"

Charlotte beamed with pride as she led him from room to room. His reaction was the same throughout the house. The room designated for his office was warm and friendly. It faced the street and he could see the campaign poster through the large windows.

"Am I living a dream or is this really happening?" Grady asked as he swiveled the desk chair around taking in the view from all directions.

"One way to tell for sure," Charlotte said.

"How's that?"

She reached over and pinched his arm.

"Ouch!" he shouted.

"Okay. Now that we've proven it's not a dream, is there anything else you want to know?"

"Ahh, no, thank you, anyway."

"Before we conclude the tour of our new home, I have a surprise for you."

"Surprise?"

"Yep. Don't you like surprises?" Charlotte asked.

"I do… if they're good ones."

"I'll let you make that decision. Come on."

Grady followed Charlotte up the wide staircase to the second floor. She led him to a closed door and paused before opening it.

"Okay, come on." Grady said. "The suspense is killing me."

Charlotte opened the door and stepped into the room. Grady followed her. "What's this?" he blurted.

"I believe it's called a nursery," Charlotte replied and searched his face for reaction.

"A nursery?" After a moment, he added, "Are you trying to tell me something?"

"It's official. Our baby is due to arrive in April."

"Oh, my! Our baby. You're sure?" Grady stammered.

"I'm sure—the rabbit died," Charlotte said.

"Rabbit?"

"Never mind, just take my word for it."

Suddenly, like coming out of a fog, it hit Grady. "We're going to have a baby!" He cried and grabbed Charlotte into a tight hug. "I'm going to be a daddy."

Charlotte pushed back. "Easy, Slugger. You're squeezing the breath from me."

Grady gently released her and led her to a rocking chair. After she was seated, he went down on one knee, and said, "This is the best day of my life." After a pause, he asked, "Is it a boy?"

"Don't know. What if it's a girl?"

"Doesn't matter." Then taking Charlotte's hand, he said, "I amend my former statement. The day I met you was the best day of my life."

• • •

Suddenly it was November and election day was upon them. The excitement in the air surrounding the Penwell family and circle of friends was almost tangible. Grady's constituents were so sure he was going to win, they planned a celebration party at the high school gym as they waited for the results.

Charlotte's father assumed the role of master of ceremonies. Standing on a raised platform at the front of the gym, using a blackboard and chalk, he posted the numbers as they came in. By 7:00 p.m., the time the polls closed, it was apparent Grady was going to win by a landslide. When Grady's numbers overwhelmed the opponent, Grady was hoisted up on the shoulders of one of the brawnier men and paraded around the gym amid shouting and singing *He's a Jolly Good Fellow!*

Grady was all smiles when his entourage deposited him on the platform at the front of the gym where Charlotte's father had been keeping score.

"Speech! Speech!" the crowd cried in one loud voice.

Anticipating victory, Grady had prepared a short speech for the occasion. He took center stage and held up his hands to quell the din. After several minutes, the rambunctious attendees finally quieted down.

"Beating the incumbent is not something I expected. Him being antiwar and me having fought in World War II obviously gave me the edge. I'm used to be on the front lines fighting for liberty and justice for all. Sitting back and waiting for everything to drop into my lap is not in my genes. Solving problems before they occur has been and will always be my quest. It will always be God, country, and family. Why do I place country above family? Because the greatest good for the greatest number will always be my goal. We'll all do well if our state does well. And if all the other states follow suit, our nation will remain great. One of my father's favorite mantras is, 'The whole is only as good as it's parts.' Our state will once again be that shining beacon on the hill!"

After the victory celebration, when Grady and Charlotte were home alone, he confessed to her that it was all so surreal, he could hardly believe it was happening—and still had trouble accepting it.

"You know what they say?" Charlotte said. "The cream always rises to the top!"

Chapter Eighteen

The Mallard Lake Connection

Grady paced back and forth in the hospital waiting room. Every so often he would poke his head out into the corridor hoping for some news. When nothing happened, he retreated and continued pacing. Charlotte's father sat quietly thumbing through a magazine as they waited for Baby Penwell to make an appearance.

"You're going to wear yourself out, Grady," Charlotte's father finally said. "Take a seat and tell me what's going on in the political arena."

"Sorry," Grady said. "I just can't relax knowing what Charlotte's going through." Then looking pensive, he asked, "You think everything's okay?"

"Yes, I'm sure it is. She's in good hands. In fact, her doctor is the same one who delivered her twenty-some-odd years ago—and look how she turned out!"

"He must be close to sixty by now, so that's not much consultation," Grady mused as he stared at the doorway.

"Yes, and also has all those years of experience under his belt."

"You make a good point," Grady smiled. "Want to get a cup of coffee?"

"No way. You're already wired. You don't need to add caffeine to the mix!"

Just as Grady sat down across from his father-in-law, a nurse appeared in the doorway. "Mr. Penwell?" she asked.

Grady jumped to attention. "Yes, that's me."

"Congratulations! You're the father of a beautiful baby boy—"

"A boy!" Grady interrupted. "We have a son! Lloyd, did you hear? It's a boy…"

Before Charlotte's father could answer, the nurse asked, "Would you like to see him?"

"Yes, yes, I would. But first, how's Charlotte?" Grady asked.

"She's weary but ecstatic. She has the baby with her, you can see them both."

Grady's legs suddenly began to shake and he felt lightheaded.

"You okay?" the nurse asked, taking his arm.

"He's okay," Charlotte's father said. "He's experiencing *first* baby syndrome."

Turning toward the door, Grady beckoned to Charlotte's father. However, Charlotte's father hung back. Although he was eager to see Charlotte and his new grandson, he didn't want to intrude on this very special moment in their lives.

When Grady entered Charlotte's room and saw her holding their son, everything began happening in slow motion. Charlotte smiled and held their son up to him. When Grady took the baby in his arms, angelic music seemed to come from nowhere. *Am I dreaming?*

Grady took the baby in his arms, and his heart soared when his son opened his eyes and appeared to smile up at him. Grady sat down on the chair next to the bed and putting an arm around Charlotte, he drew her close. Words were not necessary.

• • •

The days, weeks, and months passed in a blur. It seemed impossible, but Alexander Grady Penwell, better known as "Alex," was celebrating his first birthday. Grady's parents flew to Helena to participate in the festivities. On the day of the occasion, the scene was bedlam. The Penwell house was filled with family and close friends, including their friends' children.

The party dragged on for a couple of hours. However, when the children began to get fussy, the parents decided it was time to leave. After everyone said their last goodbyes, Grandma Penwell had the pleasure of bathing Alex and rocking him to sleep. The other adults cleaned up an array of wrapping paper, party favors, fingerprints on every surface, and toys strewn about. Luckily, the spilled drinks and squished cake were confined to the linoleum floor in the kitchen.

Collecting the trash, Grady asked, "We have to do this every year?"

"Oh, no," Charlotte said. "Only the first twelve years. Teenagers wouldn't allow parents to sponsor a birthday party. That would be disgusting!"

Grady groaned.

• • •

After Baby Alex was tucked in sound asleep, and the cleanup crew had finished their job, they assembled on the back patio. "I have something to run by you," Grady said.

His voice was so serious, every eye was immediately focused on him. "What is it?" Grady's mother asked with more than a hint of concern in her voice.

"Well," Grady began, "my term as representative is expiring at the end of the year. I think I've made a good name for myself by being on the right side of major issues and helping pass some landmark bills."

When Grady paused, his mother reached over and patted his hand. "Yes, you certainly have, and we're proud of you," she said.

"Thank you, Mom." Clearing his throat, Grady

continued, "Only recently, I learned that one of Montana's state senators, Justin Turnbull, announced he wouldn't be seeking reelection. I've been thinking about running for his seat."

Charlotte gasped. She didn't see that coming. Realizing she was shocked, Grady took her hand, "The reason I didn't mention it to you sooner is because I wasn't sure I wanted to go that route until today. Being with all of you and our friends made me realize we need to secure the future—especially for our children." After a pause, he added, "I think I can make a difference."

Charlotte's father coughed. "Ahh, I've been in this business for a long time, and by damn, I agree with Grady. I think he can make a difference. For what it's worth, Grady, you have my support."

Charlotte's father's comments roused the others out of their trance. Suddenly, it seemed like everyone was talking at once. Grady directed his attention to Charlotte. "What do you think?" he asked.

Looking squarely into his eyes, and having recovered from the shock, Charlotte said, "I'll always be in your corner if you're right. I think it's an excellent idea. Someone must step up and you've got the personality, ability, and intelligence to do so."

Blinking back tears, Grady asked, "You realize I'll be out of town and maybe out of state for long periods of time?"

"It comes with the territory," said Charlotte. "I'm willing to sacrifice for our state and ultimately our country."

And so, it was decided. The new campaign was geared toward Grady's running for the Montana Senate.

• • •

Life became hectic; it was almost impossible to keep pace. Time passed so quickly, it seemed to Charlotte as though she was turning to a new month on the calendar almost every day. Alex thrived, he took his first steps, and with Charlotte's encouragement, he said his first word, "Dada."

At dinner one evening, Charlotte pointed to Grady and whispered to Alex, "Dada." Alex turned toward Grady and shouted, "Dada!"

Grady was so surprised, he dropped his fork and jumped up, knocking his chair over. "Did you hear that! Alex said 'Dada,'" he shouted. Grady's reaction was so unexpected, Alex became frightened and began to wail. Grady picked his son up and comforted him. Looking at Charlotte, he said, "Don't know how I'll be able to leave the two of you for long periods of time if I win. I'll miss so much…" He became choked up and couldn't finish his thought.

Charlotte, the voice of reason, said, "That's true. However, don't look at it as a choice between us and our country. Remember, when you announced, we decided you could make a difference and make our country a better place for all of us. Success comes with sacrifice!"

"And behind every successful man, is an intelligent woman," Grady said. Handing the baby to Charlotte, he continued, "You continue to be my inspiration. Thank you for keeping me focused. I've been truly blessed."

• • •

Even though it wasn't a surprise, Grady once again won by a landslide. After all, he was the golden boy. Mounting the podium, before giving his acceptance speech, Grady reached out and beckoned Charlotte. Carrying Alex, Charlotte approached the stage.

"Come up here." Grady took Alex from Charlotte's arms. Alex swiveled his head, apparently not knowing what to think about all the commotion. When Charlotte was at Grady's side, Grady held up his hand to silence the crowd. He then took the microphone and said, "I'm honored to have been elected your Senator. I will serve you to the best of my ability. I'll never quit working for you and the good of the nation." Turning to Charlotte, he continued, "However, no man is an island. I seriously could not have done it with this woman at my side. I want you to meet my rudder, my compass, my port in a storm, and most importantly, my heart and soul." Grady held up Charlotte's hand and the crowd went wild.

• • •

The Penwell legacy continued and Grady ultimately served a total of four terms as senator. He acquired the reputation of making good decisions, and having done so, sticking to his guns. Even under pressure, he didn't back down to the opposition. Charlotte often said, because of the way he liked to argue his case, he should've been a lawyer. She was proud of his many accomplishments.

The Penwells looked forward to the Senate's adjournment for the August summer break. As soon as Alex was old enough, they would spend a month at Mallard Lake. Grady's Aunt and Uncle Thornton, now in their eighties, were unable to enjoy the outdoors like they used to. Thurman's arthritis and Vivian's osteoporosis hampered their ability to get around outside. Vivian complained, "It's not fun being cooped up all the time and not being able to enjoy the lake." Not wanting to sell the property, they encouraged Grady and his family to use the lodge.

After Miranda's father died, her mother refused to go to the lake. "It's haunted by too many memories," Miranda's mother said. "Your father loved it there and I can't bear to be there without him." At her mother's insistence, Miranda and Ben also spent a lot of time at the lake. Miranda and Charlotte coordinated their trips to Mallard Lake and alternated hosting dinners. It was only natural that the two couples would become close friends.

The Royes' twin girls, Sandy and Mandy, were now five years old. They had a second set of bicycles that were stored at the lodge. They biked around the perimeter of the lake several times a day. They had several board games and educational toys at the lodge. They loved Alex like a brother and delighted in playing with him and teaching him new things. The girls, had taken swimming lessons and were excellent swimmers. However, they weren't allowed to swim in the lake without adult supervision.

• • •

One afternoon, as the three children frolicked at the edge of the water, Alex lost his balance and fell into the lake. Even though he wasn't very far from the shore, he was unable to stand. Mandy panicked and rushed to help him. However, because of his wet clothing, he weighed almost as much as she and she was unable to lift him. As the two of them thrashed about in the water, Sandy ran screaming toward the lodge. Miranda was outside sweeping the deck and became alarmed when she heard Sandy's cries for help. When Sandy came into view and Miranda saw her frantic condition, Miranda threw down the broom and rushed to meet her. All Sandy could do was to point to the spot where the other two children went into the water.

Miranda closed the distance between the lodge and the lake in record time. Seeing Alex and Mandy lying on the shore, Miranda rushed up and knelt beside them. She could see their chests slightly moving, both children appeared to be breathing. Relief suddenly washed over her and she couldn't restrain the tears. Making a sign of the cross, she whispered, "Thank you, God, thank you."

Grady and Ben were making repairs on the outside of the lodge when they heard the commotion. Panting from the exertion, they were soon on the scene. Ben immediately examined the children. When Ben touched them, Mandy began to stir and Alex opened his eyes and stared up at Ben. "They both appear to be okay," Ben said, and his voice cracked with emotion. "What happened?" he asked.

Sandy stepped up. "We were throwing rocks in

the lake, and…and Alex stumbled and fell into the water. Mandy went in after him."

Mandy, now fully alert, sat up. "Mommy," she said excitedly, "a pretty lady brung us out. She… she walked on top of the water."

All four adults looked at each other. *Irene*?

THE LEGEND OF MALLARD LAKE — JUDITH BLEVINS & CARROLL MULTZ

Epilogue

Alex?

Alex, like his father, was public service minded and after graduating from the University of Montana's Blewett School of Law, he was hired by the Lewis and Clark County Attorney. He proved to be a talented attorney and was well respected by his peers. He soon acquired the reputation of being unbeatable in the courtroom. When he ran for the term-limited current County Attorney's seat, he won by an overwhelming majority. He now had the best of both worlds. He could administer and continue to stay in the trial arena.

Alex also shared in his father's love for flying. Together, Grady and Alex purchased a plane that seated up to five people. The larger cabin allowed the family to fly to Mesa a couple of times a month to visit Grady's aging parents. Sandy and Mandy, the Roye twins, would often accompany them on these excursions.

It was apparent that both Sandy and Mandy had a crush on Alex. Close friends would speculate on which twin Alex would pick. However, Alex looked upon the twins as his older sisters. His heart belonged to another. He had fallen in love in the second grade with Rita Palmer, a petite, brown-eyed, raven-haired beauty. Alex never wavered in his adoration of Rita, even though she didn't show any interest in him. Suddenly, everything changed when they started high school. Rita began to flirt with him and Alex was on cloud nine when she accepted his invitation to accompany him to the homecoming dance. After that, the couple dated almost exclusively.

Destiny intervened when Alex started working for the prosecuting attorney. When he felt like he could offer Rita a secure future, he proposed. She accepted.

Miranda and Ben?

Miranda had quit working when Sandy and Mandy were born. Now that the girls were through school and living on their own, she accepted that she was no longer needed to take care of them. Having become bored with staying at home, she began volunteering several days a week at the various charities located around Helena.

Miranda found volunteering to be very rewarding and looked forward to helping the less fortunate. Miranda's mother often complained to Miranda about Miranda being exposed to God knows what. Miranda had long ago broken free from the control her mother lorded over her. She just ignored her mother's protests.

• • •

Ben was now CEO of Helena General Hospital. Miranda marveled at his ability to juggle so many balls. Responsible for the entire functioning of the facility, he made the final decisions on, not only the daily operations, but strategy, policy and finance as well.

Ben was also active in the Knights of Columbus organization and named Man of the Year on two different occasions. Despite the demands on his time, he always had time for Miranda. He never faltered in his love for her, nor she for him.

And Tulla? Although getting up there in age—no one knew how old she was, and it was rumored Tulla didn't even know—she was still part of the family. Being crippled by age, she was unable to perform household duties, and not expected to. Over Tulla's protests, Miranda and Ben insisted she continue to live with them in the Victorian. They designed a suite for her on the main floor consisting of a bedroom, sitting room, and bathroom.

Miranda never faltered in her love for Tulla, nor did she for Miranda.

Charlotte and Grady?

Lamenting having not been involved in much of Alex's life, upon completing four terms in the Montana Senate, Grady retired from public service at age 62. Over the years, Grady always managed to attend milestone events in Alex's life. And even though he was there for every important event whether it was grade school, high school, college, or law school, he knew he still missed too much. After careful reflection, Grady decided he had made a difference when he entered public life and was able to forgive himself for being an absent father most of Alex's life.

• • •

Charlotte's father, although infirm physically, was still mentally as sharp as ever. Unable to live alone, Charlotte and Grady, after much discussion over the nursing home option, convinced him to come live with them.

"I don't wanna be a burden," Charlotte's father protested.

"You're not a burden, you're my father," Charlotte chastised. "Besides since Alex left, and with Grady gone so much of the time, it's comforting having a man around to deter would be burglars."

"I'm sure I'd put the fear of the Lord in those

burglars!" Charlotte's father snorted.

• • •

Soon after Grady retired from public life, Charlotte's father died. He was a veteran, having served his country in the First World War and his request was to be buried at Arlington National Cemetery alongside his fellow vets.

Family and friends gathered around the gravesite to say their final farewells to Lloyd Lancaster. Alex and Grady stood one on each side of Charlotte. Sensing Charlotte was having difficulty controlling her grief, Grady put his arm around her shoulders and pulled her close as tears cascaded down her cheeks.

"I'll miss him," Charlotte mumbled.

Cradling her, Grady said, "I can't take his place but I'll aways be here for you."

Willard and Irene?

As the years came and went, more incidents involving sightings of Willard and Irene were reported. The old-timers delighted in regaling newcomers with the legend of Mallard Lake. However, the miraculous rescue of Mandy and Alex always topped the list of stories told. Some listeners gasped in wonder; others raised their brow with skepticism.

When millionaire Paul Ledstone heard of the phenomenon, he surmised a hotel would thrive on the lake because of its mysterious history. He immediately purchased several acres of lakefront property and built a breathtaking hotel, The Mallard Lake Inn. The hotel even provided excursions on plush yachts around the lake. The tour guides would slow the yacht as they pointed out the special places of interest—especially the area where Mandy and Alex were rescued.

The hotel and its amenities provided hundreds of jobs for people living in the area. As its popularity expanded, Mallard Lake became a household word. It was told that some honeymooners bypassed Niagara Falls in favor of Mallard Lake.

• • •

Whether real or imagined, incidents of Willard and Irene sightings are still being reported. What do you think?

About The Authors

Judith Blevins' whole professional life has been centered in and around the courts and the criminal justice system. Her experience in having been a court clerk and having served under five consecutive district attorneys in Grand Junction, Colorado, has provided the fodder for her novels. She has had a daily dose of mystery, intrigue and courtroom drama over the years, and her novels share all with her readers. In addition to the ten novels in **The Childhood Legends Series**®, she has authored or co-authored thirty-three adult novels.

Carroll Multz, a trial lawyer for over forty years, a former two-term district attorney, assistant attorney general, United States Commissioner, and judge, has been involved in cases ranging from municipal courts to and including the United States Supreme Court. His high-profile cases have been reported in the **New York Times**, **Redbook Magazine** and various police magazines. He was one of the attorneys in the **Columbine Copycat Case** that occurred in Fort Collins, Colorado, in 2001 that was featured by Barbara Walters on **ABC's 20/20**. He recently retired as an Adjunct Professor at Colorado Mesa University in Grand Junction, Colorado, where he taught law-related courses at both the graduate and undergraduate levels for twenty-eight years. In addition to the ten novels in **The Childhood Legends Series**®, he has authored or co-authored thirty-five adult novels and eight books of nonfiction including his recently released handbook entitled **Testifying in Court—A Guide for Peace Officers**.